D1522127

Fallin' For a

Boss 2

By: Lucinda

John

Dedication

This book is dedicated to my mother R.I.P Celina John; I promise my mission in life is to make you proud. I love you!!!

Acknowledgements

God is good all the time and all the time God is good!!!! I am living proof of that statement. First and foremost, I would like to thank the Lord almighty for everything that He has done for me. It was Him that blessed me with this creative gift, and I am grateful to know that part of my purpose is to bring entertainment to people.

Secondly, to Kamauri, Kaiden, and baby Khy; you guys are my world. The strength of you guys love is the fuel to my fire. I am blessed to have three wonderful boys that call me mommy.

Next, Charles, my father, the guy that went through a lot with me; although, we may not always see eye to eye thank you for always being in my back corner. I love you!

To my number one fan, thank you for always supporting me. It was you who gave me my inner thug with all that thugged out music we be listening to in the car. LOL!! Thank you for also buying so many of my books and gifting them out.

To ALL my FAMILY and FRIENDS (too many to name) thank you for being all supportive, thank you for even pretending to support me, I appreciate it. LOVE ALL OF YOU.

I will also love to thank my fans, it was because of you FFAB part one was such a hit. I was happy to see my first book hit the charts, receive 5 star reviews, and receive all the love it did. You guys are awesome!!!!

Last but not least, I would like to thank MYSS SHAN, the best publisher in the world. Thank you for pushing me to the next level. Thank you for always being there if I need to ask you something, vent, or even need ideas. You're so hands on with us and I love you for that.

To my sisters at Shan Presents, I love you all. This sisterhood that we formed is filled with love and a bond so strong. I wish all of you ladies nothing but success. SP4L!!!!!!!!!

Text **SHAN** to **22828** to stay up to date with new releases, sneak peeks, and more....

Chapter 1

Lala

Feeling warm hands rubbing gently on my belly, I opened my eyes and saw the love of my life standing over me. I had to close my eyes and reopen them just to make sure that my eyes weren't deceiving me.

"What did I tell you about all that crying?" he said climbing in bed with me.

"I thought I wasn't going to see you again," I whispered not believing I was actually in his arms again. He took my hand and placed it over his heart before he spoke.

"My heart beats for you and our unborn baby. My life would not be complete if I didn't have you two in it. I'm here now, and I'm not going anywhere."

Pulling me on top of him, he grabbed me by the back of my head and stuck his tongue in my mouth. I savored the taste of Aqua fresh and weed letting me know he'd just recently brushed his teeth after smoking a joint.

"Mmmm," I moaned feeling him grab a handful of my ass. He flipped me over and positioned his head between my legs. In one quick motion, he snatched off my shorts and devoured my insides.

"O-O-O-Ohhhhhh shit!" I yelled out in pure bliss as he ate me out with so much passion. Latching onto my clit, he sucked it until it became sensitive to the touch. Sticking two fingers in me while making love to my pearl with his tongue, he brought me to my fourth orgasm. I was ready to tap out.

"Damn you so wet," a female voice said, snapping me back to my hurtful reality. This had been going on since I'd been captured. I would dream of being with Stacks, but once I woke up, it was a female sexually assaulting me. Sitting up, I quickly closed my legs.

"Don't be like that. You know you were enjoying it," she laughed pulling me closer to her.

"STOP!" I frantically cried, fearing she would stick that strap-on in me again.

"What the fuck are you doing?" a voice I knew all too well yelled out.

"Chill the fuck out, I'm just having some fun with the bitch before we kill her ass."

"So, when did raping her become a part of the plan?" James asked.

"I didn't know a woman could rape a woman. By the way she was all into it, that ain't sound like no rape to me."

"Whatever, just leave her alone."

"What you mad the pussy doesn't get wet for you anymore?" She laughed and walked towards the door. "Never mix business with pleasure, love will get you killed." She winked before walking out the room.

"You ok?" James asked sitting a suitcase on the bed.

"If you're going to kill me, just hurry up and do it!" I yelled in his face.

"Shhh, Lala, just calm down. You know I would never do that to you."

"Then why are you holding me here against my will? You don't do that to someone you love," I began crying.

"A doctor is coming to check on you and the baby. Trust me, Lala, we will be a family again," he whispered before handing me a few bags out of a suitcase.

"Go get yourself together," he said before leaving the room.

It felt like I had been held here against my will forever. I didn't know whether it was night or day that was how confined they had me. I was stuck in this bedroom that had an adjoining bathroom. A queen-sized bed, a dresser, and a TV were the only things that furnished the room.

The majority of my days, I would sit in the corner and draw. James knew drawing was one of the things I loved to do, so he bought me a sketchpad and a few pencils.

Getting off the bed, I walked to the bathroom. Plugging the tub up, I filled it with warm water before pouring some bath crystals in it. Once the water was nice and warm, I got in and allowed my body to relax a little bit. Picking up the soap, I lathered my body with the Olay body soap James loved so much. The smell of the lavender instantly made me nauseous.

Thinking back on the day, I was kidnapped; I wished I had never opened the door...

A knock on my door and a scream caught my attention. I wanted to ignore it, deep down inside something told me to ignore it, but when I saw a lady there with her baby, I couldn't. I thought of my baby and how I would want someone to help us if we were in need. Against my better judgment, I opened the door. Once I realized the baby the girl was holding wasn't real, I felt something go over my face and a strong scent hit me, knocking me out.

When I finally came to, I was lying on a bed in a room. I tried to open the door, but there were no doorknobs. I walked to the windows they all were bored. The only thing I had access to was a bathroom. Feeling defeated, I sat on the floor and cried for what seemed like hours before someone finally opened the door.

"Why the fuck would you do this to me!" I yelled at the man I used to love.

"Lala, calm down. Trust me, I'm not going to hurt you or the baby."

"Trust you, James? All I ever did was trust you and you let me down every single time, so why in the fuck would I start trusting your ass now?"

By now, I was in his face trying to smack some sense into his ass.

"I'm going to let you calm down, and I'll be back," he said walking out of the room and locking the door behind him.

I sat in the room for a few days with no food. The only water I had was from the sink. I would drink the water to keep myself from being dehydrated. If this was James' way of thinking he would get mind control over me then, he had another thing coming. While lying on the bed, I heard the door unlock.

"James, you are one sick bastard!" I yelled out.

"No, honey, try again," a female voice replied. Jumping up, I saw a beautiful woman with a devious smirk on her face. From that day on, she would come in and sexually assault me. I would block out the *assaults and imagine it was Stacks making sweet love to me.*

"Lala the doctor will be here soon." James' voice boomed through the intercom invading my thoughts. I drained the water, rinsed my body, and exited the tub. Looking in the mirror, I could see a change in my color. My beautiful, vibrant skin was dull and pale. My hair was a mess, and my nails were so bad I had to bite the acrylic off of them.

Putting lotion on my body, I put on a black panty and bra set, then slipped a cream colored dress on. Brushing my hair into a messy bun, I put on the earrings Stacks bought me as a just because 'I love you' gift. I was grateful James' spiteful ass didn't get rid of them.

Walking back into the room, I picked up my sketchpad and began to jot down a note. Once it was completed, I folded the piece of paper, placed it in my bra and waited for the doctor to come. After a few minutes, I heard a knock on the door. A short older lady walked in the room pushing a cart.

"Hello, my name is Dr. Rosa and I will be checking on your little one today," she spoke in an angelic tone with a smile on her face.

"Can you urinate in this cup for me, please?" She handed me a clear cup, and I made my way to the bathroom to give her a sample. "So how have you been?" she asked when I returned with the cup filled with pee.

"I'm good," I replied, keeping it short. She checked my weight and blood pressure, while she scribbled notes in a green folder.

"Okay, let's see how far along you are. Lay down for me please." I laid flat on the bed and lifted my dress up to my chest. She squeezed a cold, blue gel on my stomach, and she used the Doppler to locate my baby.

"There goes that precious sweet child," she smiled at me while pointing to the baby.

"You are eight weeks now. Let's listen to the heartbeat."

My baby's heartbeat filled the whole room bringing tears to my eyes. Moments like this were supposed to be shared with Stacks.

"Lala, I am worried about your blood pressure being high. I also found some protein in your urine that concerns me as well. I am going to schedule another visit for you in two weeks, if nothing changes then we might have to have you go to the ER for further evaluation," she said while scribbling more notes in the green folder. I burst into tears crying my little heart out. I needed her to get close enough to me so I could set my plan in motion.

"Aww don't cry, Lala. It's going to be okay," she said giving me a hug. Seizing the opportunity, I slipped the note in her coat pocket. I silently prayed that she was kind enough to get into contact with Stacks for me and let him know I was alive and well, sending him to my rescue.

"You have to stop stressing," James said looking in the green folder the doctor left.

"Shut the fuck up!" I rolled my eyes at his dumb ass. "If you took me back to my man then, I would be stress-free," I snapped.

"Well, get that shit out of your head because that nigga is dead! You either get with the program or join his ass!"

"Well, go pick out my casket now because I would rather be dead with the man I love than alive with the man I hate," I spat making sure my words were as sharp as swords. I wanted them to cut him real deep. As soon as he left, I broke down crying. I hoped what he said was a lie. Was Stacks really dead?

Chapter 2

Stacks

Sitting on the black, suede couch Lala decorated my man cave with; I sipped on some Hennessy watching Amanda sleep on the monitor. Ever since I found her instead of Lala, she'd been living with me. A part of me wanted to believe she knew more about the exchange gone wrong, but my gut told me she was innocent.

Pouring another shot, I drowned it and studied the way she slept, from the back she had a figure like Lala. However, up close they looked nothing alike. Lala was breathtaking. Her beauty spoke volumes. She had more than just a nice body; she had it all. On the other hand, Amanda was just okay in the looks department. Her body was what probably drove guys crazy.

Thinking about my baby was making me go crazy. All I did was smoke, drink, and kill niggas I thought had anything to do with her disappearance. Bear was the number one person on my shit list. As soon as I caught up with that nigga, I was going to give his fat ass a tummy tuck.

"Yo," I answered my ringing phone.

"What's good my nigga." Ralph greeted me.

Ralph, Bear, and I used to be as thick as thieves back in the day. When we were in our teens, we decided to rob a Bodega. Ralph got caught and took the fall for it by himself. Already on strike three, landed him five years in prison. He was recently released, and I felt like he was the only one I could trust.

"Nothing, just stressing my boy." I threw the shot glass across the room and decided to drink straight from the bottle.

"I feel you cuz, I'm fucked up over this, too. You are my fuckin' brother. You were the only one that held a nigga down when I was locked up. You even looked out for my kids, bruh. I owe you."

"Nah, bruh. We fam."

"No, phone calls yet?" he asked referring to the burnout phone Lala's captors left.

"Nope. Nothing." I felt so defeated.

"What you want to do?"

"We gonna continue to bleed the block until my wife is home alive."

"Bet. I'ma swing by later with some money I got for you."

Since Bear disappeared, I had Ralph take over for me and so far he was doing a better job.

"A'ight bruh, be easy," I said hanging up the phone.

Walking over to the bar, I grabbed me a bottle of Jack Daniels. I stopped to admire a picture I had taken of Lala when she wasn't paying attention.

Taking a swig of the strong liquor, I allowed myself to travel back to the worst day of my life...

BRRRRNNNNNNNGGGG!!!

"Hello?" I answered the burnout phone that the kidnappers left.

"By now, you should have figured out that we have your girl. If you want her alive and still pregnant, I want five million dollars in two weeks. I will be sending you instructions. Make sure you follow them. One fuck up and I swear I will personally give your bitch a C-section right after I beat her pussy up unmercifully," the unknown voice replied. I tried to make out the voice, but I couldn't due to the auto tune he was using. Hell, it could have been T-pain who kidnapped my wife for all I knew. Five million dollars was chump change to me. So I had no problems getting in contact with my financial advisor and having him withdraw the money for me from one of my offshore accounts.

The day of the drop, I had to make a five-hour drive to Tallahassee. Once I got there, I checked into a hotel and text the random person; Done. While waiting for further instructions, I took and shower and rolled me a fat blunt. I laid back on one of the chairs that was on the balcony and fell asleep.

BRRRRNNNNG!!!

The phone rang waking me up.

"Hello?"

"I see you finally made it. I want you to drop the money off in the blue dumpsters at Lincoln High School. I will text you the address. You have two hours and make sure you are alone. My men are watching, and if you bring a soul with you, your bitch will die."

CLICK!!

I made sure the five duffle bags were secured in my back seat before sitting in the car waiting on the address. The drive was forty-five minutes away, so I arrived early just to check out the scene. Nothing really looked out of place, so I got out, put the bags in the blue garbage can and made my way back to the hotel. I texted 'Done' and waited for a response.

"We got the money. Once we verify the money is real and is the right amount then, we will give you the girl."

Two weeks later, I was contacted and informed the trade would take place in three days. I got in contact with Ralph and had him round up a few men. I was not going into a gunfight with a knife. I ran down the plan with my men and waited for the time and place to go pick up Lala. The day of the pick up something didn't feel right, but I was determined to bring wifey home, so I ignored it. I was ready to catch some bodies, and I wasn't playing.

Walking inside of the warehouse, I spotted a woman tied up to a pole. I knew it was Lala from the back because the frame was the exact same as hers. I ran towards her. When I realized it wasn't her, a bullet grazed my shoulder and the other hit me in the leg.

I hit the emergency button on my phone alerting the men to rush in. Pulling out the guns I had in the back of my pants, I was feeling like Arnold Schwarzenegger in that movie Terminator, my guns were talking for me. The warehouse was dimly lit, so I could only make out shadows.

I took cover behind a wall and quickly loaded up my guns. Once I heard my goons letting off a few rounds, I went back in. Three bullets hit me, and that still didn't stop me. I was still walking on them niggas with straight gunplay. I felt my body getting weak, but

I was still trying to push through these niggas. They needed to feel my pain.

"You good, Stacks?" I heard Ralph ask me before everything went blurry, and I fell down. "Boss man you good?" one of my goons asked.

"K-k-kill them niggas and get the girl, if she's still alive," I stuttered before everything went black.

"Did you hear me?" Amanda asked trying to get my attention.

"What I tell you about wearing my wife's clothes?" I yelled.

The only person I wanted to see rocking those too short, boy shorts was Lala.

"Sorry, I didn't have anything to wear. Want me to take them off?" she smirked.

"What do you want?" I asked getting up to grab another bottle from the bar.

"You know you shouldn't drink so much."

"Is this what you came up here for?" I asked taking a swig of a new bottle of Jack Daniels.

"No. I came to tell you I made lunch for you. You've been drinking on an empty stomach," she said sounding so sincere.

"I'm good."

"Well, can you at least eat something? I'm worried about you."

"Ok." I shrugged just so she could get out of my face.

I wasn't trying to be rude, but my mind was all fucked up and the only thing that could calm me down was knowing my girl and baby were both okay.

After finishing my bottle, I decided to go downstairs. Amanda was sitting at the table eating a salad.

"Is that what you made for lunch?" I asked laughing.

"Well, I made this for me, your lunch is in the microwave." She smiled before stuffing another fork full of lettuce in her mouth. I opened the oven and unwrapped the food. As soon as I began to unwrap the food, my stomach began to cry out in hunger when the smell of the shrimp and fish tacos hit me. I grabbed a bottle of water out the fridge and sat down across from her.

"This is really good," I complimented her while taking a bite of the tacos.

"Thanks. I use to work at Red Lobsters, so I stole most of their recipes."

"Can you make the biscuits, too?"

"Hell yeah!" she said and we both laughed.

When we finished eating, I did the dishes while she rolled a few blunts. I grabbed her a bottle of wine and myself a Heineken. We sat by the poolside to smoke and drink.

"Let's go swimming," she said out of the blue.

"Nah, I'm good," I replied taking another pull on the blunt.

"Okay then."

She stood up and undressed until she was as naked as the day she entered the world. The hair on her pussy was shaved to form a pair of lips.

"Like what you see?" she smirked before jumping in the water.

After watching her swim a few laps in the water, I got up to take a cold shower and sober up.

Five minutes into my shower, I felt the shower door slide open.

"What the fuck are you doing?"

"Shhh," she said before getting on her knees and swallowing my dick.

"Fuuuuuuuuuuuuuuuuuuck," I yelled out as she used her tongue ring to play with the head of my dick.

She sucked me gently yet firm. Feeling my nut build up, I rammed my dick deeper down her throat and like the champ she was, she didn't gag once. I fed her all my babies and she happily swallowed them. She got off of her knees and walked out as quickly as she came in.

Damn!

Chapter 3
Bear

Riding around in my ivory and black 2014 Lamborghini, blasting Young Thug's Lifestyle, I was loving life. I just got brains from one of the baddest bitches in Dubai and I was about to go home and smash twins. A nigga was really living.

At first, I was mad James' punk ass was able to get to Lala first, but it was all good though. I was still able to get some money out of Stacks' ass by making it seem like I had her. The night I went to kidnap Lala, James already had her, so I planted a note and phone in the house to set Stacks up.

The night of the pickup that nigga was supposed to be dead, but those dumb ass niggas I hired couldn't even kill a fly with a fly swatter. I had Tasha go work with James, so she could take care of the situation. No matter how bad I wanted to do the honors myself there were too many hits out on me, and I wasn't taking that chance.

"Hello?" I roared into my ringing phone.

"Man this nigga is bitching up," Tasha huffed.

"What you mean?"

"I knew he had no intentions to kill the bitch. He had a doctor come check on the baby."

"Did he tell you why?" I asked rolling a blunt.

"For insurance."

"Insurance on what?"

"To insure once he contact Stacks, he'll believe he has Lala for real since the first time was a set-up."

"You think he's lying?" I asked taking a long pull of the blunt.

"Hell yeah. I think he plans on killing Stacks, taking Lala, and running off with the money."

"Keep a close eye on him, if he jumps wrong body his ass. We don't need him anyway," I said hanging up the phone.

*****

Pulling up to my two story five bedroom three bathroom villa, I parked my car in the driveway and made my way inside. The sight of the twins walking around my kitchen ass naked made a nigga dick hard.

"We missed you daddy," Thing one purred sitting a plate of food on the table.

"I did too," Thing two co-signed pouring me a stiff glass of Vodka.

"I missed y'all fat asses, too. Go get cleaned up for daddy, I'll be up there in a minute," I replied slapping them both on the ass.

The jiggle effect was something serious. The chicks in the U.S had nothing on these healthy booty bitches in Dubai. I sat back and enjoyed the Ghuzi (Roasted lamb with rice and vegetable), another thing I loved about Dubai was how good the food was. A nigga could eat, so I ain't have no problem trying new shit.

Drinking down my cup of Absolute Vodka with an X pill, I poured me another cup and rolled a blunt. These freaky bitches had the stamina of a horse. I needed the extra effect of the pill to keep my ass going.

Walking in the playroom, I saw Thing One's legs draped across the edge of the hot tub and Thing Two's head was underwater eating her out. I ain't know if this type of shit was legal in this country, but I ain't give a fuck hell if they liked it, I loved it.

I stood there watching, slow sipping on my drink and smoking the blunt. I could already feel the effect of the weed, liquor, and pill plus my dick was already at attention ready to salute a bitch.

"Come join us daddy," Thing Two said coming up from under the water and now sucking on her sister's breast. I wasted no time taking off all my clothes and jumping in with them.

Once I was laid back comfortably, Thing One took the blunt out of my hand, inhaled the smoke, and blew it in my mouth. I inhaled the smoke, released it out my nose, and stuck my tongue down her throat. Thing Two climbed on the edge of the hot tub and squatted in front of my face while Thing One's head went under water to suck my wood.

I sucked her pussy; matching the rhythm while I was getting my dick sucked too. When I felt my nut building up, I gripped Thing Two's ass, shoved her pussy deeper into my face, and feasted on her kitty making that shit squirt all in my mouth and nose.

Relocating to the bed, Thing Two handcuffed my hands to the bedpost. They took freaky to another loved. She pulled out a Magnum XL, shielding my dick before she slid down on it.

"Ohhhh daddy damn." She moaned as every inch of me hit her all in her chest. For a big nigga, I knew my dick game was insane.

"My turn," Thing One said as she slid down on my dick and rode me like she was in a rush to get somewhere.

"Oh damn, do that shit," I groaned feeling myself about to bust a fat one. Feeling my dick go stiff she pulled off the condom, and they took turns sucking my dick until I blew down Thing Two's throat. Being the freaky bitches that they were, they tongue kissed and swapped my nut from one mouth to the other.

"Uncuff me and let me beat that shit up!" I demanded.

"Why is my brother still alive?" Pablo's voice boomed through the room freezing me in place. I clapped my hands to turn on the lights and was face to face with the most ruthless nigga ever.

"Apparently, the dumb ass you hired isn't doing his job right," I said lying back in the bed, grabbing a pre-rolled joint from behind my ear, and lighting it up.

"What do you mean?" He asked.

"James is taking longer than expected to carry out on the plan and it seems to me that he doesn't want to kill the girl."

"I don't give a fuck! Look how lovely I have you living. I'm the reason you're in here fucking twin sisters! All I want is my nigger brother dead! First, you fail to kill Paco, now this. What kind of man are you? You useless piece shit!" he spat with venom.

I felt the back of my neck get real hot. I wanted to murk his ass and show him I could kill, but I decided against it.

"I want my brother dead now, or I will personally kill all of you motherfuckers on my own," he said.

"Just chill," I said, "It will be done. I WILL GET IT DONE! Come smoke one and get your dick sucked," I laughed waving his ass off.

"I'm serious, Bear!" Before walking towards the door, he said, "Oh and I have your sister sucking my dick. She does a great job at it." He smirked before slamming it behind him.

My phone started beeping, and it was this freaky bitch I had fucked earlier. I texted her to let her know to make her way to the playroom. I had to think of a plan quick, but first I had three pussies I was about to knock out the frame.

Chapter 4

Ashley

'James, I am supposed to be at the doctor's office in thirty minutes you better be on your way!' I yelled, leaving another voicemail for his dumb ass. I knew he was all booed up with Lala's ass. He thought I didn't know he had the bitch. He planned to skip town with that hoe. My REAL baby daddy already put me up on game. I was so over James' dumbass. He and Lala's days on earth were numbered.

In the beginning, I was in this to win the heart of the man I loved, but now money was the motive. If I rolled with my original baby daddy, then this bastard child and I would be set for life. All I had to do was stick to the plan and eliminate my targets.

Dressing in a pair of skinny jeans, a black blazer with a white tee under it, I slid on my black wedges and admired myself in the mirror. I had to admit, this baby made my already fat ass fatter. I rubbed the small baby bump and smiled down at my meal ticket. My baby was going to be my ticket to the good life.

"Took your ass long enough," I said hearing someone who I assumed was James walk into the room. I sprayed my body with my J-Lo perfume and applied a light coat of cherry bloom lip-gloss.

"Where are you going?" the biological father of my child asked. Turning around, a smile came across my face as I admired his sexy ass. "To the doctor's office with James." He walked over to me and wrapped his arms around my waist. We looked so good together. He was like the milk in my coffee.

"You need to hurry up and do as planned, so I can move you and our child to Cuba," he said licking my earlobe.

"I know, and I'm on top of it," I replied melting in his arms.

In the beginning, he was against me having his baby, but once he realized it would be his firstborn son, he had a change of heart. He was the one who planted the bug in my ear to off James' ass. Pablo was a paid nigga, and we would be better off with him than with James.

"Have you heard from your brother?" I asked breaking away from his embrace to finish preparing myself for my doctor's appointment.

"Yes, he should be coming down to see Paco this weekend."

"Do you think Paco will wake up while he's there?"

"No, I paid the nurse a good amount of money to make sure he stays in that coma," he assured me.

"Good because if Paco wakes up then he is going to expose us."

"Don't worry my little pregnant butterfly, he won't," he said pulling me close to him and serving me his tongue. The night Pablo and I met was the night James beat me and kicked me out of the car because he claimed I was all on Stacks' dick.

"Why you let him beat on you like that?" he asked me handing me a cloth.

"It's no big deal I guess." I shrugged accepting the cloth and holding it to my now broken nose.

"Do you need a ride home?"

"No, I'm fine. I'll just catch a cab." I didn't want James to see me pull up to the house with Stacks' brother.

"Well, at least allow me to give you my number and if you need anything, I'm just one call away." I handed him my phone, and he programmed his number in it.

"Call me," he said making sure I was safely in the cab as he watched it drive off.

From that night on, we began to communicate. He took me out on a few dates. Then the fucking began.

With Pablo, we never used any protection, so when trying to get impregnated by James failed, I just pinned Pablo's baby on James. I wasn't in love with Pablo like I loved James, but since James wanted to be stuck on stupid for that dumb bitch, he deserved everything that came his way. It was fuck me, now its fuck you. The baddest bitch always got the last laugh and soon I'd be laughing my almost rich ass to the bank.

"What's so heavy on your mind?" Pablo asked zipping up his pants. Sex with him was lame as fuck. He was able to get a quickie in, and I didn't even feel nothing. Hell, I didn't even know we were fucking. I was so lost in my thoughts. I didn't even feel his little dick slide in me.

"Nothing daddy, you know good dick always shuts a bitch up," I lied getting up and walking to the bathroom to clean up.

"I'm out of here, but I'll be back later. Don't forget the plan," he said grabbing his car keys and walking out the door.

"Okay," I simply said rolling my eyes. I got in the shower and washed his scent off my body.

*****

"Oh, shit I ain't hear you come in." I was startled seeing James sitting on my bed.

"You rushing me and your ass ain't even ready!" he snapped.

"I'll be ready in a few minutes," I said dropping my towel and putting on a new pair of undies.

"Leave them off and come here," he ordered.

I strutted over to him and climbed on top of him. Who said I couldn't get some good dick before I killed him?

Chapter 5

Stacks

For the past few days, I'd been driving up to the hospital to sit with Lisa. I was hoping and praying she would wake up out of the coma so she could give me information on Bear's whereabouts. I stopped at the gift shop and picked her up another dozen of roses, a few 'get well soon balloons' and a bear. I did this every day I came to visit because I knew Lala would have done the same thing.

"How are you today, Judy?" I greeted the front desk lady as I signed in to get my visitor's badge.

"Hey big daddy," she smiled while winking at me.

"You look beautiful this morning," I complimented the old sweet lady that had this crush on me. It was kind of funny because she reminded me of my Nana.

"When you gonna stop playing with me big daddy?" she asked handing me the blue badge. I grabbed her hand and kissed it.

"You're too much woman for me," I laughed.

"Stop it now," she blushed.

"Have a great day, Judy," I said before walking away.

"You just missed her," The daytime nurse said before I got to Lisa's room.

"What do you mean?" I asked confused.

"She woke up out of her coma last night. Her brother came to pick her up this morning. He had her set up to be taken care of at home by one of our nurses."

"Do you mind pulling out the chart so I can see where she's located?" I asked.

"No sir, that's against the hospital's policy, I could lose my job." I pulled out my checkbook and wrote her a check. I slid it over to her and waited for her response.

"I'll be right back," she said walking to the back room. A few minutes later, she came back with a manila folder and handed it to me. I nodded and made my way to my car.

*****

Pulling up in front of the address that was listed in the record, I sat back and waited for some type of movement. A few minutes later, I saw a nurse go in the house and another come out. I assumed they were switching shifts. I made sure I had my nine on my hip before exiting the car. Knocking on the door, I eased my hand on my piece just in case shit was about to pop off.

"How may I help you?" A nurse with a strong Spanish accent asked.

"Hey, cariño cómo vas a hacer hoy," (Hey sweetheart how are you doing?) I asked her showing off my dimples.

"Soy bueno. Cómo estás?" (I'm good how are you?) she replied while blushing.

"Que estoy haciendo bien. Estoy buscando mi amiga Lisa está ella aquí?" (I'm doing ok. I'm looking for my friend Lisa, is she here?) I asked her flashing her a smile.

"Y-y-yes," she stumbled over her words. Her eyes roamed over my body and I could tell I had her. I could charm cupid out of her bow and arrow any day. I was that nigga.

Walking into the house, it was a neatly furnished house I asked, "¿Hay alguien más aquí?" (Is anyone else in here?)

"No," she replied leading me to the room where Lisa was held.

"What took you so long?" Lisa asked as soon as we walked in the room.

"I asked you to bring me a fucking soda five minutes ago!" she snapped not noticing I was in the room as well.

"Is that how you speak to the help?" I laughed letting my presence be known.

"What the fuuuuuu……Stacks?"

"In the flesh baby. How are you feeling?" I asked taking a seat next to her.

"Besides my ribs hurting every time I breathe, I'm good. Where's Lala?" she asked looking around.

"I have something to tell you."

I didn't know how she was going to take it because Lala and her were so close.

"Don't tell me no fucked up shit, Stacks, for real." Lisa winced in pain as she tried to sit up in bed.

"Lala is gone."

"Gone where? To the nail shop?" she quizzed.

"No. Gone as in kidnapped."

"WHAT THE FUCK YOU MEAN KIDNAPPED?!" she yelled jumping out of bed a little too fast and stumbling over.

"Lisa, calm the fuck down and chill out before you hurt yourself."

I tried to reason with her, but all hell broke loose.

"What the fuck you mean calm down? Oh my God, Stacks we have to find her. Did James do it? I know his punk ass did it! I'ma body that fuck nigga myself," she rambled on like a mad woman. "Where's Bear? Is he helping you? Is that why he hasn't been to see me?" she asked.

I knew she really cared for Bear, and that was why I hesitated to answer her questions.

"Stacks, are you fucking deaf?"

"Lisa, chill the fuck out and watch your damn tone when you talking to me."

I had to put her in her place because she was getting out of pocket.

"Bear is gone."

"Gone? So what, motherfuckers are disappearing now? What, they kidnapped his ass, too?"

"I believe he had something to do with Lala going missing. He skipped out of town, and then all of a sudden she's gone. This shit ain't adding up right." I shared my suspicions with her.

The room went silent for a second. She got up and walked over to a safe that was behind a dresser. Putting in the code she pulled out a 9mm pistol. I know she was Lala's best friend and all, but one wrong move and I was sending her ass to hell.

"Well, if that's the case, then I'm ready to body that fat bitch," she replied loading up the gun.

I could see the pain in her eyes and I could tell she was hurt. I grabbed her and held her.

"Why me?" she had asked before she broke down in my arms.

I wanted to cry, too, but I had to be strong for her. The man she fell in love with was a snake. I knew the feeling all too well.

"What in the fuck is going on here?" A man walked in the room with a mean mug on his face.

My reflexes kicked in and I pushed Lisa to the side and pulled out my gun.

"Stacks, chill out this is my brother, Jimmy, Jimmy this is Lala's boyfriend Stacks." She introduced us to avoid me having to put one in his dome.

"What's good partna?" I said lowering my gun and placing it in the small of my back.

"Hey, what's up?" he asked, shaking my hand firmly.

"Any word on Lala?" he asked.

"No," I sadly replied.

"I've been doing a little investigation and I think I'm on to something."

"What the fuck have you been investigating? Did you know Lala was missing and didn't tell me?" Lisa asked ready to charge her brother.

"Sit down before you hurt yourself. I think we all need to have a seat," he said pulling out a chair and sitting down.

"I was hired by Ashley, Lala's ex-boyfriend's side bitch to kidnap and kill Lala. At first I didn't know it was Lala. A guy I do business for referred her to me, and I took the case. The day she gave me Lala's picture and information, I wanted to kill her, but I had to find out who she was working with first.

Ashley is too sloppy, and she isn't capable of pulling this off herself. The plans were for me to kidnap Lala and hold her for safety. They asked me to make it look like she was dead until I was able to assassinate everyone involved. The day I was supposed to pick up Lala I got word from an informant of mine that Lisa was in critical condition in the hospital. I decided I was going to come back for

Lala the next day and went to go check on Lisa. I had no idea there were multiple people after Lala," he said as he pulled out a folder from his book bag.

"These are the people who are somehow connected to the disappearance of Lala."

I grabbed the folder out of his hand and took a look at the pictures. I wasn't surprised to see Bear's photo, but the pictures of the next two people I saw baffled me.

"What fuck!" I yelled throwing a chair across the room. My own flesh and blood, Pablo? My brother is in on this shit, as well? What confused me was what in the world did Tasha have to do with this. The wheels in my head started turning and all I could think about was Donna. Did they have anything to do with the death of her and my twins? I couldn't believe the snakes were right under my nose the whole time. People I loved and trusted were the ones who betrayed me.

"I'll check up with you later," I said unable to be in that house any longer.

"Stacks?" I heard Lisa call my name before I jumped in my car.

*****

"You okay?" Amanda asked following me up to my room.

The whole ride home I tried to rack my brain to come to an understanding as to why my own brother would want to plot against me. Ignoring her, I grabbed a duffle bag and started packing some clothes.

"Are you going somewhere?"

"Yes," I said keeping it short. I called up Zen and told him to fire up the jet.

"When are you coming back?" she asked getting on my nerves.

I don't know why I kept her here I had no use for her ass. Once I returned, I was making it my business to put her up in her own spot.

"When I'm done handling all my business!" I snapped as I walked out of the room, leaving her ass there. I had so much on my mind. I had to get the fuck out of that house before I murked her ass off of impulse.

*****

The flight to Colombia was a blur. I didn't even know we hand landed until Zen was shaking me to let me know I had reached my destination.

"To what do I owe this visit?" my dad asked meeting me at the front gate.

"I need a reason to come see my Pops?" I asked embracing him.

"No, but you're my son and I know there is a purpose for you being here. I know you're not taking a break from finding Lala to take a vacation," he lightly chuckled while firing up his cigar. I watched the swans swim in the lake that decorated the front of the house.

"We have to talk," I said still watching the swans swim peacefully.

"Walk with me," he said as we walked towards the back of the mansion where there was a huge maze garden.

"What's going on?" he asked taking a seat on the gold bench.

"It's Pablo. He had something to do with Lala's disappearance." I sighed putting my head in my hands.

"Are you sure?"

"Yes," I answered him.

As much as I didn't want to believe it, the proof was in the pudding. He was on camera. There was no denying that my baby brother was after me, but why?

"I knew it would come down to this," he finally said after a pregnant pause.

"What do you mean, Pops?"

"A while back, I caught Pablo going through my papers in my office, and I think he came across my will. In it, I left you the cartel. You are to run things. In the event that you are unable to fulfill your duties, it would be passed down to Paco," he sighed. "Pablo is a hot-headed boy, he moves off of impulse. He does not have what it takes to run my business. I worked too hard to have him ruin things. If he has anything to do with Lala, then it confirms my suspicions of him hurting Paco."

"You know what I have to do?" I regretted those words coming out of my mouth, but that was the only way to deal with snakes.

"You have my blessing," my father said getting up. "Make sure you see Paco on your way out," his voice cracked as he spoke.

I know he was hurting behind this and I was too.

"Hola señor," the daytime nurse greeted me.

"Hola enfermera Anna," (Hello Nurse Anna) I replied taking a seat next to Paco. I watched her inject something into his IV bag. She gave me a smile, then left the room.

"Nigga, you need to wake the fuck up out of this coma I need you," I spoke putting my head down. "It's so much going on and I'm lost."

Real niggas didn't cry, but the tears started to fall when I realized how fucked up my situation was. A nigga betrayed me, my wife was missing, my brother was fighting for his life and I had to kill my other brother. Shit was fucked up on so many levels.

After an hour of silence, I was about to leave until I felt the bed shift. Looking up, I almost lost my damn mind when I saw Paco looking straight up at the sky with tears coming out of his eyes.

"Paco?" I was ready to get up and call the nurse until he grabbed my arm. He pointed to the pen and a piece of paper that were on a nearby table. I gave it to him, and he began writing. Five minutes into writing his letter his body began to seize uncontrollably. His eyes were rolling in the back of his head, and he was foaming at the mouth.

"Nurse! Nurse! Nurse!" I yelled out, but she never came.

"What's going on?" my father yelled running into the room. When he took a look and saw what was happening to Paco, he immediately pulled out his phone and called for a paramedic. Paco's body finally stopped shaking, but his eyes were closed. I placed my two fingers on his neck in search for a plus but came up with nothing.

My dad looked at me with sad eyes pleading for there to be a pulse. I shook my head no, and he broke down crying. Saying a quick goodbye prayer to my brother, I noticed the note on the floor. I picked it up and started reading it. The more I read, the more my blood pressure rose and threaten to explode.

"FUCK MAN!" I screamed punching multiple holes in the cream colored walls.

"What is it?" my father asked. I couldn't respond. It felt like someone was deflating all of the air out of my body. Picking up the note, my father began to read it.

Pablo has been paying a nurse to inject my IV to avoid me from waking up. I've been up for weeks now pretending I'm still in a coma. Bear is still alive, and he's who shot me after I discovered he was trying to kill you. Bear is responsible for Donna's death, and Pablo is paying Bear to kill you so that he can take over Papa's empire. Lala is still alive, but Bear does not have her. I'm not sure where Bear's whereabouts are, but I do know he set you up and took five million dollars of your money. He was also supposed to kill you, but I see you're too much of a warrior, and that's why he did not succeed. Lala is……

"TAKE CARE OF HIM NOW!" was all my father said after discovering the disturbing deceit his son had caused.

Chapter 8
James

I sat in the master bedroom watching the love of my life on the monitor crying her eyes out. It crushed my heart to see she was really done with me. I was ready to set this plan in motion so we could move on and start our lives over together. Just me, her, and the baby.

My only problems were Tasha, Bear, Pablo, and Ashley. I had to figure out a way to get rid of them in order to avoid killing Lala. It was never my intentions to harm her. All I wanted to do was kill Stacks and disappear with Lala and the money.

Firing up my blunt, I contemplated ways to kill Tasha. I planned on getting rid of her and taking Lala to Atlanta, Georgia. My realtor had our house ready to move in. I even had her decorate the nursery in neutral colors since we didn't know what she was having yet. My only problem would be Pablo coming after us. Once we settled in, I had to figure out a way to get to him before he could locate me.

"Spying on the bitch again?" Tasha smirked sitting on my lap. I swear I hated this bitch with a passion. I don't know what I was thinking allowing her in on my plan.

"Get off me!" I barked, letting her know I wasn't playing with her ass. Laughing, she turned around and straddled me.

"You know you like this," she whispered in my ear. "All this ass in my jeans," she sang, imitating Waka Flocka.

"Man, go on with all that." I tried to push her ass off me, but she wrapped her legs around my waist.

"Don't be like that daddy," she purred, making my dick hard. I ain't gonna lie shawty was bad as fuck, plus this weed I was smoking had me feeling some type of way.

Her lips touched mines, and I opened my mouth granting her tongue access.

"Mmmm," she moaned, deepening our kiss.

I felt her unbutton my jeans and free my dick. Her hot box gripped my dick as she slid down on it.

"Fuck!" I groaned as my eyes rolled in the back of my head.

I don't know if it was because I was under the influence, but her pussy was feeling good as fuck. Her pussy was so wet. With each thrust, I made she leaked on me.

"You like that daddy?" she asked speeding up her pace.

"Oh fuck, I'm about to nut!" I roared, feeling like a volcano that was ready to erupt.

She sped up. She was slamming her pussy into my dick, riding me with no mercy. I felt something cold on my dome, but I was too focused on catching my nut to pay attention. As she rode me faster, I felt myself having an outer body experience. For some reason, everything I ever did in life flashed before my eyes. Erupting my hot lava in Tasha, I saw Lala's beautiful face flash across my mind before everything went black.

Chapter 9
Stacks

I wanted to put a bullet in Pablo's head as I watched him kneel before Paco's casket putting on a show like he really gave a fuck. I was going to deal with his ass, but not here. Today was the day I had to celebrate the homegoing of my brother.

Paco's funeral was held at Las Lajas Cathedral, the most luxurious church in Columbia. Walking up to his pure gold casket, I felt my knees get weak. Amanda draped her arms around my waist in an effort to comfort me. I was glad I flew her up here to be with me during my time of grieving.

Paco looked sharp as ever in his pure white and gold Armani suit. I chuckled to myself. If he were able to see himself now, he would have approved of his apparel. I closed my eyes and prayed my brother's soul would safely make it to heaven. Bending down I whispered, "No te preocupes hermano voy a vengar su muerte," (Don't worry brother I will avenge your death.) in his ear, before kissing him on the cheeks and walking away.

Being a pall barrier in my brother's funeral was the hardest thing I had ever had to do, but it was tradition. If you had any brothers, they would be your pall barriers. The ride to the gravesite was very painful for me. I partially heard what the pastor had to say as I watched his body disappear into the ground. I pulled out my gold money clip and scattered twenty thousand dollars on his casket, and everyone else followed. This was another one of our traditions.

After the ceremony was over, we headed back to the house for a celebration of death. The house was decorated in white and gold with pictures of Paco everywhere. A slide show of his life was displayed on the large 92-inch projector.

"Are you hungry?" Amanda sweetly asked bringing me a plate of food.

"No, I'm good," I replied, taking in her appearance. She was looking really nice in the black and gold Gucci dress I bought her. It snuggled her body as if she had a blanket wrapped around her on a cold winter day. It was funny how money could upgrade you. A few days with her living my lifestyle had completely transformed her.

"Let me know if you need anything," she said before walking off and leaving me to have a moment alone.

I decided to join my dad who was out on the balcony nursing a drink.

"How are you holding up, Papa?" I asked pouring myself a drink.

"Not so good, Son," he paused looking at me with tears in his eyes. "Not so good." His voice cracked as he spoke. I embraced him and allowed him to fall apart. From the corner of my eye, I could see Pablo watching us. Not once did a tear fall from his eyes.

"His funeral is already planned, whenever you're ready." My dad said giving me the okay to kill Pablo. I had already made plans to do it before I left Columbia.

"Voy a cuidar de ella esta noche," (I will take care of it tonight.) I replied, downing my drink and pouring myself another one.

***

Dropping Amanda off to the hotel, I made my way to the boat to meet up with Pablo. He was under the impression that we were going to have a business discussion about splitting up Paco's cut of the business. Little did he know, I was sending him right to hell. I chose to meet with him on the boat so the sharks could devour his body once I was done with him. A snake like him wasn't worth the money of a proper burial.

"My dear, brother how are you?" Pablo greeted, giving me a hug.

"Just trying to wrap my head around everything," I replied.

"So, how do you want to split Paco's share of the business?" he asked, getting right to the point.

"Is that all you're worried about?" I was disgusted with his ass.

"Business is business," he shrugged.

I didn't have time for the small talk. I was wasting too much precious air conversing with his ass. I pulled out my gun at the same time he pulled out his.

"This is how you do it now?" I asked, glaring at him. If looks could kill, he'd be buried next to Paco right now.

"Great minds think alike, huh?" he laughed.

"Why? Why are you doing all of this shit? We're brothers!"

"Everything was supposed to be left to me. From the moment you came into our lives, you stole the spotlight. For some reason, Papa favored you. I felt like he had something to prove to you because he missed so much of your life, but what about us, huh? His sons who had lived under the same roof with him since birth! When I read his will and saw that he thought I was not worthy to take over the cartel, I decided to show him. With you two out of the way, I'd kill him and everything would be mine!"

POW!

Pablo's head split like a watermelon that had been squashed as the bullet pierced his skull. I looked behind me and saw my father standing there with a gun.

"I couldn't allow you to carry around the burden of killing the only brother you had left," he finally spoke after ten minutes of silence.

"I would have handled it, Papa!" I snapped.

"I know, Son. Let's go home. It's been a long day, and you have a flight to catch tomorrow."

"What about the clean up?"

"My men will be here soon to burn him."

Sleep in peace Paco, I silently prayed as we left the murder scene.

Chapter 10

Tasha

"Did you handle it?" Bear asked on the other end of the phone.

"Yes, it's done."

"Good girl. Do you think you can hold it down with her for a few days or do I have to send security?"

"I got it, Bear, damn!" I yelled, getting aggravated at his lack of confidence in me.

"I'm just asking. This is an important move for us, so we got to be smart about it," he said. I could hear a chick giggling in the background, which was pissing me off. Fucking with Bear, I was going to become a serial killer. Killing all the hoes he called himself wanting to fuck with.

"Who the fuck you over there ake-ke-keing with, Kenneth!" I went from 0-100 real quick.

"Tasha, hold that down for me and I'll be out there in a few days. DON'T FUCK IT UP!" were his last words before he hung up the phone to entertain whatever bitch in Dubai that had his undivided attention.

*****

I decided to go down to the little room that held Lala and have a little fun of my own. It was something about that bitch I couldn't get enough of. She was definitely cut from a different cloth than most females, including me. She just had this aura about her that made you want to be up in her headspace 24/7. Oh and that super soaker she held between her legs, good lawd! It was like she had a fountain of Fuji water pouring from between her legs.

"Rise and shine sunshine," I said, slapping her on the ass. I watched it jiggle like a bowl of Jell-O. My mouth instantly started to water, and my stomach began to rumble. I was ready to let my mouth play 'Hunger Games' between her legs.

"James, is no longer here to save you," I giggled, noticing her eyes shoot towards the door ready for that nigga to come save her. "We can have all the fun we want with no interruptions." I licked my lips and began to undress.

The tears that were running down her face did not faze me one bit, I was going to get that pussy whether she was down with it or not.

"STOP!" she yelled, kicking me in the jaw with force.

She caught me off guard, and I was kind of dazed for few a seconds. When I finally came to and it registered what she did to me, I bitch slapped the fuck out of her.

"Oh, so you want to do it the hard way?" I taunted her between slaps. "You like it rough right?"

Slap! Slap! Slap! Slap! When I was finally satisfied, I pulled out some handcuffs and cuffed her to the bed.

"Keep on playing and I'll snatch that baby out of your womb," I threatened.

Yanking off her pants and undies, I spread her legs and started attacking her pussy as if it was my prey. She sobbed uncontrollably, as if she wasn't feeling any type of pleasure and anger me instantly.

"Shut the fuck up!" I yelled, punching her in the mouth.

"Ouch!" she yapped in pain like a wounded puppy.

Strapping the strap-on around my waist, I spit on it, and shoved it in her pussy.

"Oh, no! Stop! Oh God! Nooo!" she cried as I spread her legs wider, making her feet touch the ceiling as I ignored her pleas for me to stop. I continued to brutally murder her cat. The same feeling that came over me while I was doing the same thing to Donna returned. I felt my pussy getting wetter and with each tear she shed, the more my orgasm was building. I took the strap-on off of me and strapped it around her waist. Mounting her, I rode the fake dick until I came three times.

"That shit was fire!" I said, out of breath. She was looking at me with those sad puppy dog eyes crying like I gave a fuck. Something snapped in me as I watched her rub her belly. I unstrapped the strap-on from around her waist, lubricated it with the juices that were still flowing from between my legs, and shoved it up her ass.

"Oh, nooo!! Pleeeeease stop," she cried as I continued to violently pump the dildo in and out of her ass. I blacked out, and my mind went back to the day I told Stacks I was pregnant.

"Tasha, I don't have time to play these games with you," he said getting dressed after I broke the news about the baby to him.

"What the fuck you mean, this your baby too!" I yelled, getting in his face.

"Man get the fuck out of my face with all of that shit. Every time I fuck you, I put on my own condom, I pull out before I nut, and I flush it in the toilet. EVERY FUCKING TIME!! So, you tell me how the fuck is this fucking baby mine?" he snapped, pushing me out of his face.

He was right. The baby wasn't his. I wanted him to believe it was since Bear was in denial. Stacks and Bear were the only two men I had been with, and Bear wasn't ready for a baby. In fact, he tried to guilt me into having an abortion by saying the baby was Stacks'.

I ended up getting an abortion, but I had some complications. My uterus ruptured, and I had to get surgery, which left me with the curse of never being able to bear children again. I blamed Stacks, and that's why I made sure Donna suffered. I was repeating the cycle with Lala. If I couldn't have children, well, he couldn't either.

Feeling a liquid substance run down my arm snapped me back to reality.

"You nasty bitch!" I screamed, punching her with the same hand her blood and shit was all over. Getting up, I left her shitty ass handcuffed to the bed and went to go take a shower. Stripping down naked, I allowed the hot water to soothe my body. The thought of having Lala all to myself for a few days made my pussy jump. Unhooking the showerhead, I placed one of my legs on the edge of the tub and allowed the vibrations of the water to make me cum.

Chapter 11
Lisa

I was sitting in my new Lexus coupe waiting for Stacks to return home. I wanted to know how close we were to bringing Lala back home. I was tired of lying on my ass all day healing while my best friend was out there going through God knows what. I wasn't 100% yet, but I was close.

If it wasn't for the slight limp I had, no one would have ever known I had almost lost my life behind a crazy bitch. I swear if I ever saw that bitch Tasha again, I would dog walk her ass!

A little old lady knocking on Stacks' door caught my attention. She was dressed as if she was a nurse or a doctor. I wanted to get out of my car and say something until I saw her pull out a piece of paper from her purse and tape it to the door.

I waited until she was gone to get out of my car to retrieve it. Getting back in my car, I unfolded the paper and began to read it. Tears instantly flooded my eyes. I was mad and happy at the same time. I quickly sent my brother a 911 text along with Stacks' address and told him to meet me here ASAP!

Two hours later Stacks exited his all black BMW 328i. The windows were so dark that I didn't even know he had anyone else in the car with him until I saw him walk over to the passenger's side and open the door for a chick. Stacks was a real gentleman, but my problem was he was being a gentleman to the wrong bitch!

"Where the hell you been? I was sitting here for more than two hours!" I startled them both, jumping out of my car straight snapping.

"What are you doing here, Lisa?" Stacks asked in a calm voice. One thing about him was he was an unpredictable character. It was hard to read his emotions.

"I came here to see what was up with Lala, you know the bitch you was fucking with heavy? The one that's carrying your child! In case your ass might have caught amnesia or some shit!" At this point, I didn't give a fuck if he was a boss nigga, hell I was a boss bitch. Like my dawg Lil Scrappy said, "I ain't never scared!"

"Man, Lisa, get the fuck out my face with that shit before I snap your neck for real." He was still calm, but that bulging vein in his forehead told me otherwise.

"And if I don't?" I challenged, begging him to jump stupid. I was a certified thug, licensed to correct a nigga.

"It's not worth it, Stacks, let's just go inside," the little bitch he was with him had the nerve to say.

"Who the fuck gave your ass permission to speak?" I roared getting in her face ready to buck. I had all this built up frustration in me ready to let loose.

"You're acting really ignorant right now. The neighbors are starting to stare."

"The neighbors are starting to stare?" I said, mocking her. "Bitch you have no neighbors! You a temporary bitch, as soon as we pick up my sister, it's asta la vista for your ass. Matter of fact, pack your shit now because the HEAD BITCH IN STACKS' LIFE, LALA, WILL BE HOME SOON!" I snapped, clapping my hands for emphasis.

"Coming home soon?" Stacks asked with a raised eyebrow.

"Read it and weep," I said throwing the note at him. Out the corner of my eye, I caught the chick rolling her eyes. I looked her in the face and showed her all thirty-two of these pearly whites.

"When did you get this?" Stacks asked.

"An old looking lady taped it on your door earlier."

"Fuck!" he yelled, walking away to talk on the phone.

"Your time is up bitch! You need help packing?" I laughed, leaving her, standing there looking dumb.

*****

"We move in tonight!" Stacks exclaimed to the group of guys that were gathered at The Headquarters. This was my first time being here, and I already felt like one of the guys. We were all sitting around a huge mahogany conference table, listening to Stacks, who sat at the head of the table. To his left was this fine ass nigga by the name of Ralph, which from my understanding was his new right-hand man.

My mind wandered to Bear. A part of me still cared for him, but the hate I had for him for what he was putting my best friend through overshadowed all of that. It was always chicks before dicks, so there was no way in hell I would ever fuck with Bear after what he did.

Hell, if I saw the nigga I would kill him on sight. I was so loyal to Lala that I would do anything for her. She was my backbone, and I put it on my mother's grave that I was catching a few bodies tonight.

The drive to Port St. Lucie was a long one. We were split up in five different cars. I was in the passenger's seat while Ralph was in the driver's seat. I kept looking over at him and stealing glances. He was a sexy hunk of chocolate. Standing 6'0, he was midnight black, he had nice wide shoulders and the way his six-pack was set up underneath his wife beater had me in a trance. His hair was cut in a Lil Boosie fade, and his goatee tee was trimmed down to perfection. Catching me staring at him, he winked his eyes and licked his full sexy lips.

I was happy when we finally reached our destination. Another minute in the car with that man and I would have jumped his bones. The house where Lala was held was in the country. It was surrounded by a lot of trees. There wasn't another house in sight. Everything was all spaced out, so if Lala had tried to escape she would have been stuck.

"We don't know how many niggas are in the house. Based on the note, the lady said there was only a male and female when she came, so we have to move with caution. Do not move until I tell you to! This is the life of my wife and baby that's at risk. I swear on everything I love I will kill you and wipe out your whole family tree if you fuck this up!" Stacks said giving us a 'don't fuck up or else' pep talk.

While his men were scoping out the house, he was barking out more orders like a mad man. I had to give Stacks his props because he handled everything well. Not once did I see him break a sweat.

"Boss, there's only one person in the house," one of his goons said.

"Man or woman?" Stacks anxiously asked.

By the silhouette of the body, I would say it's a woman." I wanted to jump up for joy and scream, but I held my composure.

"Which way can we best enter the house?" Stacks asked suiting up. He was putting on a bulletproof vest and loading up his guns. While his goon gave him the blueprint of the house and ways to get in it, I watched him put a gun in a holster around his ankle, and two in the hostler around his body. Holding a gun in his hand, he looked at us and said, "Let's go in."

We entered the house from the garage door. Slowly walking up the stairs, I could smell a nasty scent of a body decaying. My heart sunk a little, while I prayed it wasn't Lala's body rotting.

"In here," Ralph's sexy ass voice spoke through the radio. Following his voice and entering the room, a smile slowly crept across my face. Looking over at Stacks, I could finally see some anger seeping out of his pores.

"Wake the fuck up!" he said, using the tip of the gun to shake her awake.

"What the FU…." The words got stuck in her throat once she realized she had a gang of motherfuckers in her room, ready to murk her ass.

"Where's Lala?" Stacks asked picking her body up out of the bed and flinging her in a chair as if she were a rag doll.

"Tie this bitch up!" he said to no one in particular. "WHERE IS LALA?" he shouted, slapping her across the face. Spitting the blood out of her mouth, she gave him a smile.

"I killed the bitch earlier," she began to laugh, and it pissed me off.

I put on my chrome plated, pink diamond brass knuckles and punched her in the mouth two times with so much force her front two teeth flew out her mouth. All she did was look at me and smile.

"Shouldn't you be dead bitch?" she asked.

"No bitch, but you will be." I went straight beast mode on her, fucking her face up.

"Enough," Stacks said, pulling me off of her.

"I found her," another voice boomed through the radio. "We're bringing her up now."

"10-4." Stacks spoke into the radio before turning his attention back to Tasha.

"Where's Bear?" he asked.

"I'm not telling you shit. You found your bitch now hurry up and kill me because you ain't getting shit out of me," Tasha said, glaring into Stacks' eyes with the same intensity he was staring into hers with.

"You think that nigga would have been loyal to you?" he reasoned, trying to get her to spill the beans on Bear, but she wasn't having it. I had to give her props because she was being real loyal to that grimey ass nigga.

"I don't give a fuck! I want to ask you a question."

"What is it?"

"Between Donna and Lala, who had the best pussy? I sampled them both, and I want to say Lala," she laughed.

Since she wasn't saying shit and we had Lala there was no reason for Stacks to entertain the bitch. I decided to use my purple, diamond, chrome plated 9mm gun to finish the bitch off. I shoved the barrel of my gun in her mouth and pulled the trigger. Her brain matter splattered all over the walls and on my brand new Timberland boots.

"I'll make sure to send your mother her black dress," I said kicking the remains of her head off her body.

"I just caught a body about a minute ago," I mimicked Bobby Shmurda doing the 'Hot Nigga'. Ralph joined in, and we started dancing around her dead body. It felt good to finally body the bitch.

"When y'all done performing, get the guys to torch this place and meet me at the hospital."

My heart broke seeing her in that condition. Stacks carried her unconscious body to the car and laid her across the backseat. She was naked, and her body was bruised. She smelled like she hadn't showered in days. Stacks sat in the back seat with her holding her in his arms. I prayed that she and the baby made it through. I didn't think I could handle life if I lost her.

Ralph pulled up to the front doors of the emergency room and Stacks immediately hopped out of the car with Lala in his arms not waiting for the car to come to a complete stop.

Chapter 12

Stacks

I was going crazy sitting in the waiting room for a nurse or doctor to come tell me my wife was okay. The condition I found her in pissed me off and I swear once I caught up with Bear and Ashley, I was going to make them feel her pain. James was already dead when we got to the house. He was lucky he died by the hands of someone else because I had every intention of making him die a slow and painful death.

"The family of Lala Williams?" the Asian doctor asked walking towards us.

"Yes, I'm her husband."

"Lala suffered a lot of trauma. She was sexually abused both vaginally and anally." She paused taking her glasses off. She sighed before saying, "There was a lot of protein found in her urine, so she has to stay here for a few days just so we can monitor her and the baby."

Hearing her say my baby was okay made me so damn happy.

"So, the baby is alive?" Lisa asked with tears in her eyes.

"Yes, the baby is perfectly fine."

"When can we go back and see her?" I asked.

"After the nurse cleans her up. We gave her some medication to help her sleep and allow her body to rest, but I'll allow you to see her for a few minutes."

We waited a few minutes before walking into her room; she was lying there peacefully. I could hear the soft, cute snoring I missed so much. Standing over her, I took in her beauty. Even with the cuts and bruises she had on her face, she was still the most beautiful woman I had ever seen. Taking off my shoes, I climbed in the bed with her and pulled her close to me.

Rubbing her stomach, I closed my eyes and thanked God for sending her and my unborn child back to me. I whispered in her ear how much I loved her and our baby before I finally fell asleep.

***

The next morning, I felt a pair of eyes staring at me. I smiled knowing that the love of my life was up.

"Hey baby," I said opening my eyes.

She started crying.

"C'mon Ma, you know how I feel about all that crying," I said as I pulled her closer to me and kissed her tears away.

"Is the baby okay?" she asked just above a whisper.

"Yes, my Lil Soulja good." I smiled and kissed her. She was a little hesitant at first, but then she finally gave in. We kissed for what seemed like an eternity before Lisa and Ralph interrupted us.

"I could kick your ass right now!" Lisa laughed with her eyes filled with tears.

"I missed you too, Lisa," Lala said, giving her a hug. I noticed Lala looking Ralph up and down, so I decided to introduce them.

"Bae, this is one of my good longtime friends, Ralph. Ralph, this is my wife Lala," I said, introducing them.

"Nice to meet you, Lala," Ralph responded, extending his hand.

"Likewise," Lala said, taking his hand and shaking it.

"Babe we got some moves to make, so I'll let you catch up with Lisa," I said, kissing her before leaving.

Once we reached the car Ralph asked, "Yo, what you gonna do about the chick at the house?"

"I got her a nice little spot, a car, and a few bands. She should be fine."

"Not that, I mean the feelings she's developed."

"Man, it wasn't even like that between us," I said, waving him off.

"You may not see it that way, but she does. Trust me. I see the way she acts when she's around you. Shawty's feeling you."

"Shut up and roll up nigga," I said, tossing the bag of weed in his lap. I knew he was right. That was why

I had to make that trip to Miami to clear shit up before wifey came home.

When we made back to Miami, I dropped Ralph off at home and made my way home. As soon as I opened the door, the aroma of food consumed my nostrils. I walked to the kitchen, but no one was in there. I could see the table was set for two, and a few dishes were on the table. I uncovered the dishes and my mouth began to water at the sight of the pot roast with vegetables and white rice.

"I see you finally made it," Amanda said, startling me.

"Yeah, I'm back. The food smells good," I replied.

"Did you find her?"

"Yes."

"Well, sit down and eat so we can celebrate."

We made small talk over dinner, but you could tell there was tension in the air.

"So, does this mean I'm homeless now?" she asked laughing, but I could tell she was serious.

"No, you're not homeless. I copped you a spot."

"Really?" she asked, shocked.

"Yes, finish eating and I'll show you."

*****

"This is it," I said, pulling in the driveway and parking the car.

"I love it!" she exclaimed, leaning over to give me a kiss. She unbuckled her seatbelt and got out of the car to inspect her new house. I tossed her the keys and waited by while she went and did a walk-through of her new home.

"Oh, my God, thank you so much!" she shouted, coming out of the house while jumping up and down like a hyperactive child.

"You're welcome. The dealership is supposed to be coming by to drop off your car tomorrow. Here take this," I said handing her a duffle bag with fifty thousand dollars in it.

"Thank you," she said again, leaning in to give me a kiss.

My mind told me I should have pulled back, but for some reason I didn't.

She tugged at my belt buckle and stuck her hand in my pants. The soft touch of her hand had my dick standing at attention. Pulling me by my hand, she led me into the house. Closing the door, she began undressing. She dropped down to her knees and gobbled my dick. Her hand and mouth were moving in a rhythmic motion as she hummed on my dick causing a vibrating sensation.

"Oh, shit!" I moaned as she slowly licked the head of my dick making my dick jump. A few minutes of the head doctor, left me emptying my seeds in her mouth. She spit the nut back on my dick before slurping it all back up and swallowing it.

I pulled up my pants, grabbed my keys, and walked back to my car. Sitting inside, I rolled up and smoked me a blunt. I sat and fought with myself. My head was telling me to get on the road and leave, but my dick was telling me to go and fuck that pussy up.

I sat and played with my thoughts a little more before reaching in the glove compartment and getting the box of Magnums. Everything in me screamed, 'Take yo ass back to Port St. Lucie to be with Lala, but instead I walked back in the house and locked the door behind me.

94

Chapter 13

Lala

Waking up and seeing Stacks, I thought my mind was playing tricks on me, but once it finally registered that it was him, and I was no longer in that hell hole, I was beyond happy. My body was still sore from the beating and assault I suffered from Tasha's psychotic ass, but I was glad it was all over.

"I'm happy you're back, Chica," Lisa said, getting in bed with me.

"Me too." I cuddled closer to her. "Are you crying?" I asked, feeling something wet on my shoulders.

"No," she replied before she finally broke down crying.

This was all new to me. I was always the one crying on her shoulder. I thought she was one of the strongest people I had ever met because I never once saw her shed a tear. I didn't know what to do, so I just held her close and we cried together.

*****

The next day, I woke up with Lisa still lying next to me and no sight of Stacks. That was really odd to me. I thought he wouldn't want to leave my side.

"Good morning cry baby," I said nudging Lisa to wake up.

"Shut up trick!" she laughed, sitting up in the bed.

"Where's Stacks?"

She gave me a look that told me she was about to tell me something that I wasn't going to like.

"Lala, you know you're my sister and I would never keep anything from you."

All I could do was stare at her. My heart started beating fast as I frantically racked my brain to see what could have possibly happened these passed two months in my absence.

"Let me put you up on game on what's been going on."

I listened to her as she told me how Tasha ran her over and tried to kill her over Bear. How Pablo,

Stacks' brother, basically orchestrated everything that took place. She went on to tell me how she killed Tasha, which I was happy to hear, and how they found James dead.

What caught my attention was when she went into detail about this Amanda character, who had been staying with Stacks for the past two months. To say I was pissed was an understatement.

"So, he has the bitch living in our house?" I was so mad that tears started to fall.

"Yeah, but trust and believe I told the bitch to pack her shit, and if she ain't gone about time we get there, I have no problem putting her ass out."

"Did he fuck her?" I asked, holding my breath for an answer.

"To be honest, I don't know, but you should talk to him first before jumping to conclusions," she tried to reason, but I wasn't having it.

"I'm going to your house when I get released."

"But La..."

"End of discussion!" I said cutting her off. While I was going through hell, that nigga was out here acting as if I didn't exist. Lisa and I talked and caught up about everything before she decided to go back to the hotel to shower and change.

Late in the afternoon while I was catching up on this new show, 'How to Get Away with Murder', Stacks decided to show his face. My heart melted and I started to smile until my brain reminded me that I was mad at him.

"What's up bae?" he greeted me, licking my lips before attempting to kiss me. I shut that down quick by turning my head and adjusting my body, so that my back was facing him.

"You good?" he asked.

"I'm great."

"You not happy to see your man?"

"My man ain't obviously happy to see me since he's been MIA."

"Really?" he laughed. "I was out tying up some loose ends."

"Tying up loose ends? Like getting that bitch out of my house!" I yelled, turning to face him. "Cat got your tongue?" I asked, after three minutes of silence.

"You fucking her?"

"No," He finally answered.

"So, what was she doing living in our house for two months?"

"Helping me find you."

"So she had to live with you to help you find me?"

"It's not like that," he stressed.

"Well, tell me how it is because I'm confused!"

"I had her stay with me to make sure she wasn't reporting to anyone. She was staying in the guest room with security watching her 24/7. I didn't want to risk letting her go if she had anything with your abduction."

"Yeah, okay. She better be out of the house by time I get home!"

"Done," he said climbing in bed with me.

"I want a new house."

"Done," he said rubbing my stomach.

"Why is your mommy snapping on daddy," he asked my belly.

"Because daddy want to be on some other type of shit," I replied.

Today was the day I was going to be released. I was happy as hell. I was ready to return to Miami.

"Okay, Ms. Williams, let's check on the baby one more time, and I'll get your discharge papers," the doctor said getting ready to give me an ultrasound.

"Looks like everything is good here. You're about twelve weeks. The heartbeat is nice and strong, and your blood pressure is better than it was when you first got here. I am going to prescribe you some prenatal vitamins and give you the paperwork to give to your doctor at your first prenatal checkup."

"Thank you, Doc," Stacks said, taking her hand and kissing it.

"No problem, I'll be back with the papers," she blushed.

I wanted to kick his ass up and down the hospital's hallway for being so damn friendly.

"What?" he had the nerve to ask.

"Keep playing with me," I replied, rolling my eyes.

"Stop being jealous," he joked, pinching my cheeks.

The doctor came back in the room with papers in her hand, "Here you go, just sign here, and here," she said, pointing to the x's where my signature was needed. She gave me my discharge papers, and I was ready to go home.

"Where's Lisa," I asked Stacks once we were in the car.

"She's back in Miami."

I adjusted my seat and leaned my head back. I prepared myself for the long drive home.

*****

"We're here," Stacks said, shaking me.

Opening my eyes, I looked out the window and noticed we weren't at home.

"We're home." he said, with a smile on his face. "Let's go inside."

Taking off my seatbelt, I followed behind him.

"Put your hand on the door knob."

I placed my hand on the doorknob and a green light blinked.

"In case of an emergency or if you don't have your keys, you can just turn the door knob and the sensor is able to detect your hand print and recognize you live here," he said, opening the door.

"SURPRISE!!!" Everyone shouted once we entered the house. The house was beautifully decorated with balloons and welcome home banners. There weren't a lot of people there, but I expected that because Stacks never really liked for people to know where he lived.

"Welcome home, Lala." Stacks' father said giving me a kiss on my hand. I laughed in my head realizing where Stacks picked up that habit from.

"Hola, Papa," I responded, returning his kiss, but on his cheeks.

"I'm glad you are home."

"I am too," I replied. "I'm sorry about..."

"No, no, no, it's okay," he cut me off. "Today is about you mi amore."

"Papa, are you trying to steal my woman?" Stacks interrupted, wrapping his arms around my waist.

"If I wanted to, it wouldn't be hard," he replied laughing.

For the remainder of the party, we laughed, ate, and enjoyed each other's company. My heart stopped when I saw Jimmy. Back in the day before James, we used to have a little fling going on before he left for the army.

"When did Jimmy come home?" I asked, pulling Lisa to the side.

"Hell if I know. All I know is I woke up from my coma, and he was here," she laughed; already knowing I had feelings for him. If he didn't leave and go off to the army, who knows what could have happened between us.

"You still feeling him?" she asked.

"No, we were young, plus I'm with Stacks."

"Uh, huh that's what your lips say."

"What's up with you and Ralph?" I asked, wanting to know why they were being extra friendly.

"Nothing, he fine as hell though."

"So, why not pursue him?" I probed.

"He has two kids."

"And?"

"He has two baby mamas."

"Ok?"

"I'm not trying to go through that type of stress," she said, sipping her drink.

"Who knows, he might be a great guy."

"You right and I'll never find out. I'm tryna see what that dick can do though," she laughed.

"You're so damn silly," I said, laughing along with her.

The party started to wind down, and everyone started to go home.

"You ready for a tour of your new house?" Stacks asked after the last guest left.

"Yes, lead the way."

The house was bigger than the one we lived in before. The living room, themed the white room, was beautifully decorated. An all-white suede sectional was in the middle of the room decorated with black and gold throw pillows. There was a huge black fireplace in the back. Walking around the room my toes sunk into the plush white carpet. I admired the tall crystal and gold chandelier. The gold statues that decorated the room were simply breathtaking.

Opening the black and gold curtains, I fell in love with my front yard.

The family room was decorated in cherry oak with a light yellow color painted on the walls. There was a big bookcase in the back of the room filled with books, a 90-inch television mounted on the wall, and pictures plastered on the opposite wall. We got into the home elevator, which brought us to the second floor. This is what Stacks called, "The Relaxation Floor".

His office was on this floor along with his man cave. My woman cave was decorated in soft pink and cream. There was an 86-inch television mounted on the wall and a mini bar in the far back corner.

"Why is there a stripper pole in my woman cave?" I asked Stacks.

"In case you and your girls want to turn up," he laughed.

He showed me the next room, which was an empty childproof playroom.

"I wanted you to be the one to decorate the playroom and the nursery," he said as we walked to the elevator and rode up to the third floor.

"This is where all the bedrooms are located," he said showing me each room. There was a total of six bedrooms on this floor.

"Here is the baby making room," he said, opening up the door to the master bedroom. It was completely gorgeous. There was a king canopy bed, his and her closets. My vanity was all diamond. The adjoining bathroom was equally beautiful. There was a shower and a Jacuzzi tub, a urinal and toilet, and his and her counter space. Opening the French doors to our balcony, I admired South Beach.

"Do you like it?" he asked wrapping his arms around my waist.

"I love it baby, thanks."

"Anything for you."

"So, what happened to the old house?" I asked, turning around and facing him.

"Chill out. I sold it."

"Just checking because I hope you ain't think I was going to let that bitch stay up in that house," I snapped, rolling my eyes.

"Keep rolling them and I'ma knock em' right out," he said, slapping me on the ass.

"Yeah, okay."

Stacks pulled me outside on the balcony. He hit play on our surround sound system, and a Charlie Wilson instrumental began to play. He got on one knee and began to sing the words of the song, 'You Are'.

"Butterflies is what I feel inside
And every time it's like my first time oo wee
And I can never find the words to say
You're the perfect girl
You're made for me
It's so easy to love you baby
We're compatible, incredible and natural we are
And girl I've never felt this way before
From the bottom of my heart
Baby girl I just wanna tell you that you are

The reason I love the reason I trust

God sent me an angel

You are the best in the world

A wonderful girl

Knowing you're by my side brings tears to my eyes"

After he finished singing the hell out of the song, he pulled out a pink rectangular diamond ring. The diamond in the ring blinded me. I had to squint a little.

"Lala, will you make me the happiest man in this world by becoming Mrs. Anthony "Stacks" Jones?" he asked, taking the ring out of the box and sliding it on my finger.

I stared at the ring with tears falling out of my eyes. Never in a million years did I think God would answer my prayers. Here I was in a beautiful house, carrying a precious baby, with the man I love. I guess it was true what they say, 'It takes having a bad man to appreciate a good one'.

"Yess!" I shouted loud enough for the whole city of Miami to hear me.

He got up and kissed me. I wrapped my arms around his neck and allowed his tongue to tango with mine.

"You trust me?" he asked sitting me on the edge of the balcony.

"Yessssss," I moaned as he slipped his hand in my pants.

"Do you love me?"

Yesssssss." I grunted as he stuck two fingers in me and made love to me.

"How much?" he asked.

"I don't know," I answered, feeling myself close to an orgasm.

"You don't know?" he said, pulling his fingers out of my soft spot, using my wetness to tease my clit.

"Well, let me remind you."

He pulled my pants down and plunged his dick so far in me I thought I was going to spit it out of my mouth.

"Mmmmmm," I moaned when he found my spot and started attacking it.

"Do you know how much you love me now?" he asked.

"No," I replied, forcing him to punish me.

My nut was slowly building up, and I knew once I got to that point, I was going to flood the city of Miami.

"Oh, Gawwwwwd!" I screamed, feeling myself getting closer and closer to that point. When I was almost there, he stopped. My eyes popped open, and I gave him that, 'if you don't put the dick back in, we gonna have some problems' look.

"I'm not putting it back in until you tell me how much you love me," he said as if he was in my head, reading my thoughts.

"I love you as far as the beach water goes times one thousand," I answered, trying to scoot closer to him. He got on his knees and ate me up as if I were a 'Hungry Man' TV dinner. My legs started to shake, and he continued to feast on my goodies until I released my juices. He slid his dick in and fucked me until I lost count on how many orgasms I had.

When we were finished, he put me down so we could wash up. I almost fell flat on my face as my legs gave up on me.

"You forgot how to take this dick?" he laughed, picked me up, and carried me to the bathroom. He adjusted the dials on the Jacuzzi tub making sure it wasn't too hot for the baby. Satisfied with the temperature, he poured a few bath crystals in the water, undressed me, and put me in the water. Undressing himself, he climbed in behind me and pulled me closer to him.

"So, you ready to tell me what happened?" he asked, grabbing a sponge and squeezing bath gel on it. As he lathered my body, I began to tell him the hell I had suffered for the past two months. When I went into detail about Tasha's assault, I felt his body tense up a bit. When I was finally done, I turned around to look at him, and his eyes were as red as blood.

Rinsing my body off, he lifted me out of the tub and laid me on the bed. Drying my body off, he grabbed the bottle of lotion and rubbed me down from head to toe. Pulling the comforter back, he laid my body on the bed. He kissed me on the lips, covered me and left the room.

I knew better than to go after him, he needed space to digest what I told him, and I intended to give him that. I snuggled the body pillow and for the first time, I was able to fall asleep in peace.

Chapter 14
Stacks

Finally having Lala home with me was the best feeling in the world. To know that her and my baby were still alive was a blessing that I couldn't thank God enough for. The traumatizing events she had to endure fucked my head up. I was on a manhunt for Bear and once I found him he wasn't going to like what I was going to do to him. I wanted to kill Ashley, as well, but she was pregnant, and her baby did nothing to deserve that fate.

Rolling a blunt, I sat back and reviewed my business numbers. Putting Ralph in charge was the best thing I ever did. We were now seeing more money than my great-great-great-children would be able to spend.

Logging into my computer, I booked us a nice suite in Columbia. My dad wanted to speak with me and Ralph about partnering up with the Lopez's family. I was down because they were doing the damn thing in Miami, and whenever I could avoid beef and make money, I would take that opportunity, especially since I was about to become a father. Paying for the rooms, I decided to go back upstairs and retire for the night, next to my wife.

***

I woke up to Lala laughing on the new iPhone 6 Plus I had bought her.

"Who are you talking to?" I asked, sitting up and looking over at the clock. It was nine in the morning, too damn early to be gossiping.

"Lisa, let me call you back, my man is up," she laughed before saying her goodbyes. "Good morning daddy," she said as she straddled me. There was no hint of morning breath. That is what I loved about her. Her hygiene was always on point.

"Morning mommy," I responded. I got up to take a leak, brush my teeth, and then got back in the bed with her.

"What's for breakfast?" she asked.

"Let's play a game. Let's do a 69 and whoever nuts first makes breakfast," I replied pulling her on top of me.

"Deal," she smiled, sitting on my face.

She swallowed my dick whole, making me scream out like a little bitch.

"I want eggs, bacon, and toast," she said before necking down. She made the dick extra wet and swallowed it again.

"Damn, slow down," I groaned, feeling my dick hitting nothing but the back of her throat. I tried to focus on eating her, but the things she was doing with her mouth distracted me. She sucked me up like I was a bottle of water then she swallowed my nut.

"I win," she said. "Go cook my food."

Not wanting to go out like a sucker, I sat her on my face and allowed her to ride my tongue until I was able to make her squirt a few times. After that, I got up and went to the kitchen to make my queen breakfast.

"Breakfast is served my lady," I said a half hour later as I walked in the room with a tray filled with food. I prepared her bacon, eggs, toast, cheese grits, and fresh fruit.

"Looks good," she said, mixing her eggs and grits before devouring them. I sat and watched her eat like a damn pig.

"Want more?" I asked as she licked the plate clean.

"Please?" she smiled stuffing a piece of bacon in her mouth. I prepared her another plate of food, cleaned the kitchen, and went down to my man cave to smoke a blunt and play 2k15 on my Xbox One.

"Yo' nigga that's a foul!" I yelled at Ralph through the earpiece I had in my ear.

"Can I play?" Lala asked sitting on my lap.

"Yo Ralph wifey want to play, I'ma get up with you later," I said, logging off my online game and handing her a controller.

"You know how to play?"

"Be quiet and pass me a joystick."

We played a good five games, and I beat her all five times. I knew she didn't want to play nor was she interested in playing, but she wanted to bond with a nigga, and I had to commend her on that.

"We're going to Columbia for a week," I told her turning off the game

"When?" She asked

"In a few days."

"Business or pleasure."

"I'm going to handle some business first, but then I'm all down for the pleasure," I said climbing on top of her.

"Can Lisa come?"

"Yeah."

"I have to call her so we can go shopping," she said trying to get up.

"Damn can a nigga get some first?" I asked, opening up her robe and sliding into my favorite place on earth.

*****

After dropping Lala off at Lisa's house, I made my way to Lil Haiti to collect money. Driving up to one of my trap houses, I saw someone that looked like Ashley. I followed just to get a good look to see if it was her. Once I got closer, there was no denying it. That was the devil in the flesh. I wanted to run her ass over, but her bulging belly is what stopped me. By her appearance, it looked as if karma had kicked her ass enough. I felt bad for the poor kid.

"What's up, Ralph?" I dapped him up.

"What's good boss man?"

"Shit, just vibing. You ready for our trip?"

"Yeah, a nigga feeling good about this shit. We gon' be making mad noise in these streets."

"For real," I said picking up a stack of money to begin counting.

"What's good with Lisa?" he asked.

"Who? Lala's Lisa?"

"Yeah, her. I'm tryna get with shawty, but she ain't giving a nigga no play."

"She probably still fucked up in the head about Bear's ass."

"You should get her to come to Columbia with us," he suggested.

"She's coming."

"Well, I bet by the time we come back home I'ma have her ass on team Ralph," he laughed, and I joined him.

Feeling my phone vibrating off the hook, I picked it up thinking it was Lala. Seeing Amanda's name pop up on my screen, I ignored the call. The phone beeped. I picked up and read the text:

AMANDA: *Stacks I need to speak with you please its an emergency.*

ME: *I'm working.*

AMANDA: *Come by when you're done, I'll be here. You know your way, use your key.*

I put the phone down and went back to work. I called Lala and checked up on her, telling her to call me when she was ready to come home. When we were finish counting the money, I was impressed.

"Tight work," I said, giving Ralph his props. For the week, he brought in eighty grand, ten more than what he totaled for last week. Giving him his cut, I put the rest of the money in the duffle bag. Lifting the back portion in my trunk, I put in the combination to the secret compartment I had installed and put the money in there locking it back up. I got in the car and drove to Amanda's house to see what was so urgent.

"Yo' I'm here, what's up?" I asked opening the door and seeing her watching TV on the couch. I had to give it to her, she wasn't using my money in vain. Her house looked real nice and cozy.

"Nice to see you finally made it," she said getting off the couch and walking towards me dropping her robe.

"Amanda, for real man, I'm not with this today," I said, frustrated.

"Please, just one last time," she begged, wrapping her arms around me.

She stole the words out of my mouth with a kiss. It was something about her that had me thinking unclearly. I carried her body to the bedroom and laid her on the bed. Undressing, I got on top of her and began kissing every inch of her body. She kept trying to get me to go down on her, but that was a no-no. The only pussy I was eating was the one between Lala's legs.

A soft moan escaped her lips as I sucked on her breast. I used my thumb to play with her clit.

"Yes daddy!" She squealed in pure delight, grinding her hips into my finger. She was so wet and warm that I wanted to feel the inside of her. I pulled down my pants and was about to put in it in her.

I just want to take you out and show you off,
You already know that you the perfect one,
Girl when I'm with you, I feel like a champion,
Ever since I got with you I feel like I done won me
a trophy,

A trophy, I won me a trophy.

Saved by wifey, I thought as I got up and answered the phone.

"What's up baby?"

"Okay, I'll be there in a few."

"Love you too," I said hanging up the phone.

Looking over at Amanda, I could see she was pissed.

"Sorry. When wifey calls, I gotta answer. I'm out. I'll get up with you later," I said, getting dressed and leaving without waiting on her response. Thank God Lala called me when she did because I wasn't thinking straight. I was about to run up in that broad raw. Thinking of all the consequences that could have come afterwards had me feeling like shit.

I sent Lala a text telling her I was outside waiting for her. Seeing all the bags in her hands, I got out and helped her.

"What? Did buy the whole mall?" I teased, putting her bags in the back seat.

"No, I just got a few things for our trip," she said, getting in the car and buckling her seatbelt.

"Shit a few things, it looks like you put somebody out of business," I laughed.

"Shut up, I got you some stuff, too," she said, laughing with me.

"Good looking out."

"Duh, don't I always got yo' back?" she asked.

"Like chiropractor," I replied, leaning over to give her a kiss. She made a face, but then kissed me back.

When we got home, she went inside and left me to carry all her bags in the house. Sitting the bags on the bed, I began undressing. I smelled my shirt and instantly noticed why Lala made that face. I smelled like fresh flowers. I hurriedly jumped in the shower hoping she wouldn't question me. Once I was done cleaning off Amanda's scent, I dressed in a pair of shorts and climbed in bed. Lala was already asleep, so I pulled her closer to me, prayed a prayer of protection, and I was out for the count.

Chapter 15
Ralph

"Amber, you really need to grow the fuck up!" I argued with my baby mama. I was dropping the kid off, and she was mad because I had my daughter with me. I ain't give a fuck though because there was no way in hell I was letting my kids grow up without being in each other's life.

"See you later, Jr," I said handing my son his book bag and giving him a pound.

"Later, Dad."

I peeled off six hundred dollars and handed it to Amber. Like the thirsty bitch she was, she counted the money and made sure it was all there. Every week I was paying her six hundred dollars, plus I was taking care of all of my son's expenses. All she did was sit home and act ratchet with her ratchet ass friends.

On the other hand, my daughter, Riley's mom was mad cool. There were no feelings between us. Laurie was a full-blown lesbian in a committed relationship until one night of drinking led to me popping her cherry and impregnating her. She didn't try to keep my daughter away from me. As a matter of fact, she would bring Riley down twice a week to visit me. At first, I was skeptical about having my daughter raised in a lesbian home, but who was I to tell Laurie who to love.

Amber and Laurie were like night and day. If I ever wanted to pursue any type of relationship,

Amber would be the one to fuck it up. She was one of those bitter baby mamas, who thought they owned you just because they had your baby.

Dropping my daughter off, I gave her a kiss and handed her mother six hundred dollars as well. Due to me being incarcerated I missed the first five years of both my kids' lives. Therefore, I was making up for lost time.

"Bye bye, Daddy," Riley said giving me a kiss.

"It's never bye, it's see you later, princess."

"Okay, Daddy," she smiled, walking inside.

I sat in the car for a few minutes before driving off.

Growing up, I never had anything. My mother busted her ass working two jobs only to come up short on the bills every month. I learned at an early age that I had to hustle in order to survive. Once I got into the game, there was no turning back. The thing about hustling was the fast money became addicting.

Anything less than what you were accustomed to becomes an insult. I was speeding through life, not making smart choices and ended up behind bars for five years. The worst part about being in jail was finding out I had two different women pregnant, and I wouldn't be able to do anything for them. That alone had me feeling like I was less than a man.

I was happy with my life. I was out of jail and making money to take care of my kids. I knew there weren't any good paying legit jobs for me as a felon that was why I went back to doing what I knew best, hustling. I wasn't about to flip no damn burgers for no seven dollars an hour.

Stacks being the generous nigga he was looked out for a nigga. He was always looking out for everyone on his squad. That was why I was confused when I found out Bear turned on him. We were tight as fuck growing up. We had a brotherhood that blood couldn't make stronger. So for someone to bite the hand that fed you deserved to pay the ultimate price, life.

Looking down at my beeping phone, I smiled at the text. It was from my daughter wishing me a good night. For her to be only five, she knew how to text and call me. As soon as I got home, I made sure everything was packed for my trip before I went to bed.

***

The following day, I woke up to my phone ringing.

"Hello," I answered, still sleepy as fuck.

"Nigga wake up!" Stacks' voice boomed through the receiver. "I need you to slide by and pick up Lisa."

"Oh, word?" I asked, trying to contain my excitement.

"I knew that would wake you," he laughed. "I'ma go ahead and text you her contact information."

"A'ight," I replied, before hanging up the phone.

Since I was already up, I decided to jump in the hot shower where thoughts of Lisa's sexy ass flooded my mind. She was a rare type of breed. She was sexy, smart and gangster as fuck. Even though she shut me down for having two kids with two different women, I was confident that I was going to have her calling me daddy soon.

When I finished my shower, I made sure my face was neatly shaved before walking to my closet and finding something to wear. I decided to put on a pair of blue True Religion jeans, a white V-neck, and a fresh out the box pair of all white Air Force Ones. Checking my fly in the mirror, I put on a little of that 'Get you wet when you get a scent of me' cologne.

I text Lisa to let her know that I was on my way to come pick her up in thirty minutes. I went as far as to ask her to have breakfast with me and when she agreed a nigga was happy as fuck.

Hitting the sensor on my six-car garage, I admired my cars. I was feeling like a hot nigga, so I decided to drive my all black drop top Camaro. Punching Lisa's address into my GPS, I blasted Rick Ross's new album, and cruised the city, if a few months ago you would have told me that I would be living like this, I probably would have killed your ass for lying.

"Your destination is on the right," my GPS, Kathy spoke.

"Thank you, Kathy," I said.

"Anytime, Ralph," the GPS replied.

I swear technology today was so advanced. Getting out the car, I walked to her door and rang the doorbell. She came to the door in a purple lace bra and thong set; the sight alone had my dick fighting to get out of my pants.

"I thought I told you to be ready in thirty minutes." I said licking my lips

"You can't rush perfection," she replied turning around and walking towards the back of her house. I closed the door and waited for her.

"Can you get my bags for me; they're in the closet by the door," she yelled from the back of the room. Opening the closet door, I was amazed at what I saw. She had a gun display mounted on the back of the wall, that shit had my dick hard. I was all down for a gangster bitch.

"You ready, because I'm hungry," she said coming out of the room dressed in a red mini dress. The leopard wedges that she wore made her legs look long and thick.

"You ready?" I asked, hypnotized.

"Ain't that what I said?" she smirked, licking those sexy lips.

I grabbed her bags and threw them in the backseat. Then we headed to Aunt Lucy's for some breakfast.

The waitress seated us, took our orders, and left us to engage in small conversation.

"Why you giving a nigga a hard time?" I asked, getting to the point.

"What are you talking about?" she innocently asked

"I mean, you see I'm tryna get with you, but you playing."

Taking a sip of her orange juice, she looked me in the eyes before saying, "One thing about me, I don't play no games. You cool or what not, but I'm not down for the baby mama drama. I would hate to be the reason that one of your kids grow up without a mother, because if a bitch jump, it's lights out for ya'. To avoid something messy, I rather we just be friend."

The waitress came and sat our food on the table; we began to eat in silence.

"Plus, you wouldn't know what to do with a woman like me," she smirked before finishing up her food. She was about to be my girl, and she ain't even know it.

After breakfast, I paid the bill and we made our way to the airport. The whole drive was a silent one, I was thinking of ways to get her on my team and she was busy texting away on her phone. I wanted to ask her who the hell was over there making her smile so much, but it wasn't my place, yet.

When we arrived, I parked my car in the parking garage and carried our bags to the back, where we would be boarding Stacks' private plane. Stacks was the definition of a hardworking man and if I could obtain half the success he had, I would be a made man.

Boarding the plane, nobody was inside. I assumed Stacks and Lala hadn't arrived yet. The pilot took our bags and we took a seat. Lisa was busy on the laptop, so I put on my Beats headphones and started listening to music. A few minutes later, I saw Lala and Stacks come from the back looking like they were up to no good. I had to smile to myself because he ain't change at all.

I remembered one time we all went to the fair and he took Donna to the back of the Farris wheel and handled his business. The love Lala and Stacks was something I was trying to build with Lisa, but hell I wasn't going to chase her ass forever.

A kiss on the lips woke me up. Looking up, I saw Lisa standing over me.

"We're here," she whispered in my ear. "Don't forget my bags."

I watched her ass sway to a beat of its own as she exited the plane.

"What's funny nigga?" I asked Stacks, who was laughing.

"Nothing," he laughed, as we finish getting the bags.

The hotel that we were staying in was beautiful as hell. Our room sat right on the beach, so I had a nice view of Columbian women ass. I dropped Lisa bags off in her room, which was right next to mine. I had to thank Stacks for that later on. I pulled out my phone and called my kids to let them know I loved them.

I spoke with Riley, but of course Amber had to be the one to give me hell and I wasn't able to speak to Jr. I was starting to hate that bitch more and more every day. I don't know what the fuck I was thinking fucking with her chicken head ass like that.

We weren't schedule to meet up with Stacks' dad until tomorrow, so I decided to take advantage of this trip. Dressed in my Gucci silk swim shorts, I headed out to the beach. As soon as I stepped foot on the scene the woman began throwing themselves at me, hey what could I say the kid was fresh. I allowed them to sit with me and we had small talk. One went as far as to give me a lap dance. I laid back in the beach chair and enjoyed Columbia's fine art.

"If you wanted a stripper, you was better off paying me," Lisa said, taking a seat next to me.

"You jealous?" I asked

"Of what?"

"This," I said, smacking one of the women on the ass.

"Never that," she said, pulling on her shades.

I could tell she was feeling some type of way and I was loving it. I grabbed my lady friends and we went and got into the water leaving her there to pout.

Chapter 16
Stacks

"Lala, how many times do I have to tell you, you ain't wearing that!" I yelled at her hardheaded ass. We were supposed to meet up with my dad for dinner and she called herself wanting to wear this short ass dress.

"It's just a dress damn!" she yelled back at me.

"Get fucked up if you want to, but you ain't going nowhere with me like that. You either sit your ass here in this hotel or change." I said, giving her an untilmatium.

"Oh, my God!"

"You can call him, but you still ain't leaving here in that dress." I was staring at her through the mirror as she undressed and put on another dress that covered up more than the first dress did.

"Happy?"

"Very! Now hurry up before we're late," I said, slapping her on the ass.

Two hours later, we finally made it to my dad's house. The maid led us to the dining room where there was already people seated having small talk.

"Hola, Papa," I greeted my father

"Hello my Son, hey my Dear," he said kissing Lala on the hand

"This is Ralph, my partner I've been telling you about and Lisa a friend of Lala's," I introduced everyone

"Nice to finally meet you young man, I heard you've been doing a lot of great things," he said, embracing Ralph

"Thank you sir, I learned from the best," He replied, returning the gesture.

"Well, let's sit and eat."

Mid-way through our meal, my dad stood and tapped the side of his wine glass with his butter knife.

"I have an announcement to make," he spoke, silencing the whole room. My father possessed so much power that everyone immediately stopped what they were doing and all eyes were on him

"I first off want to say to my son Anthony, you've made me so proud of you. I watched you transformed from a hot headed little boy to a level headed man. It is my greatest honor to announce that I will no longer foresee the cartel, I am handing it over to you." The room erupted into applause as everyone cheered and congratulated me.

Raising his hand, my dad silenced the room and began talking again.

"As you know, we decided to merge with the Lopez's'," he said, pointing to Carl and Maria Lopez. "I will also like to congratulate Carla Lopez, his father passed down the throne to her. So Carla and Anthony will now become business partners," he then raised his glass

"To Anthony and Carla."

He said giving a toast. The room followed his gesture and toast to the news, as well. As for me I sat there confused, how in the hell did he expect me to work with a woman that I used to deal with on a personal level.

"Papa, what is the meaning behind this?" I asked pulling him aside.

"I had no choice, we merged and Carl wanted one of his family members to look over his portion of his business. I had no choice but to agree," he argued

"After what Carla and I went through, that will cloud her judgment, women are not built for this!" I yelled, getting upset.

"Son, are you still feeling something for Carla?"

"No she was just something to help me cope with Donna, I mean she is a good girl, but it wasn't what she thought it was. She is a woman scorned and this can hurt business." I was trying to get my point across.

"Just do your job, and that only and things shall be fine. End of discussion!" he dismissed me, raising his hand to signal that he was done speaking on this topic. I nodded my head and walked away. Things was about to get out of control, I could feel it.

*****

Dropping the girls back off to the room, Ralph and I decided to go out for drinks.

"So, what's up with what your pops was hollering about?" he asked as soon as we took a seat in the VIP at Rio Vista nightclub.

"Man, I'm shocked. After Donna passed, I used to fuck with Carla on some friendship type shit, and then we started fucking around with each other. There was never a title, she wasn't my girl, we just had an understanding. We messed around a few times while I was in Miami, but I cut it off once I started getting serious with Lala. One day she went mad crazy, she showed up in Miami and threw a fit. I haven't heard from her, until now," I said, gulping down my drink and pouring myself another one.

"Damn fool, so what you going to do?"

"I guess I'mma ride it out and pray to God she don't start any trouble," I sighed.

"I ain't gon' lie baby bad as fuck. I know Lala gonna be pissed."

He was so right; Carla wasn't an average woman she was pretty as hell. She stood at 5'6, she had rich creamy tan skin, her long black her flowed down to her fat, round ass, her green eyes was one of her features that captured you the most. I was screwed.

When I finally made it back to the hotel, Lala was asleep. I went to go sit out by the beach to clear my head and smoke a few blunts.

"Long time no see," a sweet voice spoke

"How have you been, Carla?" I asked, inhaling deep on the smoke.

"I've been good, you?"'

"Couldn't have been better," I said, passing her the blunt.

She took a few puffs before passing it back. We had a nice little rotation going before she finally spoke. "You hurt me."

"I'm sorry; it was never my intentions to," I confessed

"I'm over it now," She lied

"Good. We don't want anything to come in the way of business."

"Do you love her?" she asked.

"With all my heart, she is about to become my life and the mother of my child. My heart beats for her," I honestly answered

"Did you love me?"

"I liked and cared for you, but it wasn't quite love. I was still getting over Donna and I wasn't thinking clearly."

"Oh I see," she replied, she started to say something but she changed her mind.

It was getting late, so I decided to take it in. I gave her the rest of the weed, wished her a good night, and went back to the room. Stripping down to my birthday suit, I jumped in the shower and allowed the hot water to massage my back. I loved Lala with all of my heart, every day with her made me believe that she was made for me. It was as if God made her personally from my rib. I was not trying to lose her over anyone or anything. If this issue with Carla was ever to escalate, I would step down from my position. No amount of money or power was worth your happiness.

"Oh, shit you scared me," I said walking out of the bathroom and noticing that she was sitting up in bed.

"I couldn't sleep," she sniffled

"Why are you crying?" I asked getting in bed with her and wrapping my arms around her.

"I'm just emotional, that's all."

"Pregnancy hormones?"

"Yes, I guess."

"Let daddy make you feel better," I said, opening up her rob. She was nice and naked underneath, just how I liked it. I positioned my head between her legs, linked her feet around my neck, and ate her out as if I was in a hotdog-eating contest.

Chapter 17

Lisa

"I'm not sleeping in here until you find that spider," I said, as Ralph was on a manhunt in search of the big ass spider that ran under the bed.

"Well, you might as well come back to my room then," he said getting off the floor. He was shirtless and wearing only a pair of boxer. I could see the outline of his dick as it played peek-a-boo through the slit. He flexed his muscles on purpose just to show off how well defined his body was.

"Are you going to stand there and drool all over a nigga or are you coming?"

"I'm coming, but you better not try anything," I said.

I was very much attracted to Ralph, but the fear of the heartbreak I suffered from Bear was what was holding me back. I wasn't really worried about the fact that he had two different baby mamas; there was no bitch on earth that could pump an ounce of fear in my heart.

Following behind him, we entered his suite. "You can sleep in this bedroom; I'll sleep in the guest room," he said walking off and leaving me in the room. I stripped down to my bra and thong set and cuddled up in his sheets. His scent was all over the bed, putting me in a daze. I battled with heart, trying to reason with it, letting it know that this guy might be different. My heart ended up telling me hell no and to erase that thought out of my head.

The smell of fresh cooked bacon woke me up out of my sleep. Sitting up and stretching, I noticed a cart filled with food and a note attached to it. I got up to read the note

Good morning beautiful,

I had to run a few errands with Stacks this morning, that is why a spider and I couldn't join you for breakfast. Enjoy.

P.S. next time you want to sleep in my room, you don't have to lie about a spider, my door is always opened for you.

Love,

Your future boo.

I smiled at the corny note, before enjoying the mini breakfast buffet. When I was done eating, I decided to go back to my room and take a shower. While in the shower, I kept praying that the spider didn't jump out on my ass. I had nothing against animals or insects; I just ain't want their asses nowhere near me.

Dressed in a long blue sundress, with a pair of gold Gucci sandals on complementing my freshly pedicured toes, I was ready to start my day. I sprayed myself with my Armani perfume and examined myself in the mirror. Giving myself the ok, I made my way to

Lala and Stacks' room to wake her ass up, so we could go shopping for tonight. Knocking on the door for what seemed like eternity, she finally came to the door.

"Damn, what took you so long?" I snapped, walking into their suite.

"Sorry, I have a bad headache," she sadly stated. I could tell there was something really wrong with her, and it was more than just a headache as she claimed.

"Seriously, Lala, it's me you're talking to. I know you don't think you're about to feed me that bullshit ass lie."

"It's nothing, really," she said getting in bed. I got in bed with her because it was a matter of time before she broke down crying. Lala was so sensitive and the baby hormones just added more to her sensitivity.

"I love you and all, but I really want to go shopping," I said after lying in bed with her for fifteen minutes. "Get up and get dressed so we can go."

"Oh, my God! I can never have peace and quiet," she pouted while getting out of bed.

"Nope!" I replied, opening her suitcase to find her something to wear.

Since she wasn't showing, I decided on a pair of True Religion shorts, a black and gold Versace crop top, and a pair of Michael Kors gladiator sandals.

Waiting for her to get dressed, I called the car service to come pick us up.

"Yesssssss fish!" I applauded Lala as soon as she walked out the bathroom. I'm not a hater I always gave props when props were due and Lala was a certified baddie. I curled her 20in Brazilian weave to perfection and made sure her make-up was flawless. She didn't want to admit it, but I could tell she was feeling a little insecure having Carla work so close to her man. Hell if I was her, Carla's ass would have mysteriously disappeared. I didn't play those types of games when it came to my man.

The driver dropped us off at Oviedo Mall, the biggest mall in Columbia that had over one hundred stores inside. Ripping through the malls, we had about fifteen bags each and we were only on store number six. In the Gucci store, I bought Lala a royal blue, laced, two piece crop top and skirt set. I also picked her up a pair of red pumps that would look perfectly with her outfit. Picking her a few accessories to finish up for her outfit, I paid the total of thirty-two hundred dollars. She was worth every penny, so I didn't mind at all.

"I'm hungry," she said once we left out thirteenth store.

"Me too, let's go to the dine-in theater."

"Ok cool, we can finally watch that new Denzel Washington movie."

We waited for the driver to come get our bags before we went in the movie theater. The host seated us and then took our orders, we both ordered chicken pasta. During the previews, I noticed Lala texting with a screw face; I made a mental note to ask her about that later on.

I swear if Stacks was giving her hell I was going to kill his ass like I should have killed James' bitch ass. Just as the movie was about to play, the host came back with our food; we ate and enjoyed the movie.

Tonight was our last night in Columbia and it was also Stacks' promotion party. His father rented out the La Bama nightclub; if you weren't on any boss type level you weren't allowed in. I checked myself out in the full length mirror; the white and gold halter-top dress I was wearing fit my body like a glove. I slid on my gold Prada pumps, grabbed my clutch

And the bag that held Lala's clothes and made my way over to her room.

Stacks answered the door looking sharp as ever in an all-white Hermes linen suit.

"Hey Stacks where is Lala?" I said, walking inside of the room,

"In bed sleeping."

"Sleeping?!" I snapped. "So, she ain't going?"

"No, she says she not feeling well, I told her I would go say 'hello' to the guest then return," he said, putting on diamond Hugo Boss watch on.

"I'll stay with her," I lied. I had every intention on dragging her ass to this party.

"You sure you want to waste a nice outfit?" he said, exaiming my attire

"Yes, it's cool."

"Ok, well call me if you need me and I'll be home after I greet my guest," he said, before walking out the room.

I waited until I heard the door beep, signaling that it was locked, before barging into the bedroom.

"Get your ass up now!" I yelled, yanking the comforter off of her body

"What Lisa!!!???" she shouted and pulled the covers back over her head.

"I don't know what has gotten into you, but you're not my Lala. So you're basically not going to go support your man on his big night, leaving that bitch to smile up in his face? Really Lala? What part of the game is that?"

"You wouldn't understand."

"Well make me then," I said, pulling the covers off of her body. Her face was stained with tears.

"She is so pretty."

"What's your point? You're way prettier than she is and I'm not only saying that because I'm your best friend. The only thing she has on you is those green eyes; hell if you want we could go buy you some contacts to solve that. There is no need for you to be insecure, you're the one he loves, you're the one with the ring, and you're the one carrying his baby. Stacks is a good guy that really loves you, I don't believe he will do anything to intentionally hurt you; that man lives for you," I lectured her.

"I didn't pick up anything to wear."

"I got you covered." I pulled the clothes out the bag and laid everything out on the bed.

*****

When we finally made it to the party it was live and in affect. The DJ was spinning *Gasolina* by Daddy Yankee and the Columbian chicks were on the dance floor getting it. I grabbed Lala by the hand, so we could show these Spanish mammies how it was done in the U.S.

Winding our hips to the music, we instantly stole the show. The perks of being a stripper was that you had the ability to dance to all types of music, I was able to shake my ass to country music if I had to. I spotted Stacks out the corner of my eyes coming towards us.

"Your man is on his way over here," I whispered in her ears.

My words were like gasoline added to her fire because she really started to show out.

Stacks came over and wrapped his arms around her waist and they began dancing. He whispered something in her ear and I saw her blush. I was glad my best friend was back to herself, because I couldn't deal with a depressed bitch. The DJ decided to slow it down, so that was my cue to exit stage left. I made my way to the bar ordered two shots of Patron and sat back and watch my best friend piss Carla off.

"Why you mad tho?" I mouthed once she noticed me watching her. She rolled her eyes and walked away. I laughed at her pathetic ass before taking both my drinks to the head and ordering two more.

"You might want to slow down before you hurt yourself."

Turning around I was face to face with Ralph. I gulped down my drinks, ordered two more then responded.

"I can hang."

"Yeah, ok," he laughed ordering him a bottle of water.

"Why you not drinking?" I asked slightly slurring my words.

"One of us has to have a sober mind, or we'll both end up in trouble," he smiled.

"What if I want to get into trouble?" I asked.

"Then you better be ready for the consequences."

I wasn't trying to hear what he was trying to say, tonight was my last night in Columbia and I was trying to turn up. On shot number seven, I started feeling myself, so I started slow grinding on him. I felt his dick respond to me, so I straddled his lap and performed for him as if he was a high playing client.

"You are playing with fire," he whispered in my ear.

"I have Neosporin in case I get burned," I replied, planting kisses on his neck.

Chapter 18
Ashley

When Bear called me with the news that Stacks rescued Lala, then killed James and Tasha, I was enraged. I had been trying to contact Pablo, but wasn't getting an answer. My money slowly started to wind down until I was officially broke. I lost my condo and my car due to me not being able to keep up with the payments. After staying with Loye for a while, I finally got approved for section 8 and was living in a rundown two-bedroom apartment in Little Haiti.

I was the type of bitch that talked down on these government assistance hoes, now I was one of them. I swear this was not over yet! I was going to make all of them motherfuckers pay one way or the other. I decided to put my cosmetology license to use and got me a job at BB's Nails. Getting out of bed, I jumped in the shower to get prepared for work. I lathered every part of my body before rinsing off and getting out of the tub.

Allowing my body to air dry, I went into the kitchen to pack my lunch for work; thanks to food stamps I had the luxury of having steak, shrimp, lobster tails, and bake potatoes. Walking into my bedroom, I applied lotion on my body, when I got to my baby bump I smiled a little.

Although in the beginning of this pregnancy, I wanted nothing to do with this child, but it was funny how attached you get to something swimming, kicking, and rolling around in you. Going in my closet, I looked for something to wear. I didn't have a wide variety since some of my things didn't fit anymore.

Deciding to wear a pair of blue jeans, I put on a white kami; tank blazer and I dressed it with my tan sandals. Applying light make-up to my face, I brushed my weave down my back, grabbed my purse and lunch bag, and then headed off to work.

The walk to the bus stop was five blocks long. When I finally made it there, I was out of breath and tired as fuck. *This part of Miami is so damn ghetto*; I thought as I sat on a dining room chair. A few minutes later, the bus finally showed up, I swiped my bus pass and took a seat in the back. It was a shame that after all Rosa Parks went through, black people still chose to sit in the back of the bus.

When I made it to work, one of my clients Amanda was waiting for me, I did her nails a few times and she always tipped extra saying that portion was for the baby.

"What's up girl?" I greeted her tying the apron around my body.

"Nothing just chilling, needing a fill-in real badly."

"You just got your nails done last week," I said. I wasn't complaining though if she was willing to spend her money, I was willing to re-do her nails everyday if I had to.

"Girl you know how it goes," she said pulling her phone out and dialing a number. I guess the person didn't answer because she hung up and tried calling three more times. On the fourth time, she decided to leave a voicemail.

"Stacks baby, I've been calling you, call me back when you get this message to let me know that you're ok."

Hearing the name Stacks had my ears perking up, so I decided to fish for more information.

"Your man ain't answering?" I asked, removing the nail polish from her nails.

"No, that nigga went on vacation with his baby mama. He returned yesterday, so I don't know why he's not answering."

"Wait, your man took his baby mama on vacation?" I questioned

"Yeah."

"And you're ok with it?"

"I have no choice but to be, they're engaged."

"So you're basically his side piece?" I asked, trying to hold back from laughing in this dumb bitch's face.

"Something like that. Lala and I are more like teammates," she smirked.

"Do she know about you?"

"Somewhat," she replied

Jackpot!!!!! I thought listening to her ramble on and on about how she met Stacks. I was flabbergasted that she would go into details about everything not even knowing who I was. That was female's problems nowadays. They were so quick to tell their hair dresser, nail tech, and everybody else their business not knowing them from a can of paint.

When she was done, I sat there with my mouth wide open. I had no idea that Bear was able to get money out of Stacks by setting him up. I didn't know why I ain't think of that first. When I was done with her nails, we exchanged numbers so we could link up. She thought she gained a new friend, but all I was really doing was using her to get my revenge.

The rest of the day flew by. I knocked off all of my clients one by one with a huge smile on my face. The taste of revenge was right there on the tip of my tongue and boy was it sweet. After closing up the shop, the owner volunteered to give me a ride home and I gladly accepted it. I texted Loye and shared with him the great news before falling asleep feeling like the happiest woman alive.

Chapter 19
Amanda

'You know what to do when you hear the beep' this was call number forty-eight, and all I was getting was the voicemail.

"UGHHHHHHHHH!!!!!!" I yelled throwing my phone across the room. I started hyperventilating. I was having a panic attack. I ran into the kitchen and grabbed a brown paper bag. I started breathing into the bag, trying to regulate my breathing. I grabbed the razor off the counter and sat on the floor. Rolling up my jeans I found a nice spot to start cutting. With every slice I made, I felt myself getting high. Cutting was a habit that I developed in foster care.

Growing up, I never had a mother or father. My mother was a crack head whore that gave birth to me and threw me in the garbage can as if I didn't mean anything to her. I was discovered by an old couple that took me to the hospital and decided that they wanted to take me in. As I got older, I became a rebel. I would get bad grades, sleep with men twice my age, and snort coke. I was basically a troubled child calling out for help; however, everyone around me was too deaf to hear.

My adoptive mother had enough of me when she caught me in her bed with my ass up and her husband behind me beating my little twelve year old pussy up. She turned me into the courts, stating that she wasn't able to care for me anymore. They sent me to live in a foster home, where the real hell began. The girls in foster home always bullied and beat on me because I had the ability to attract guys with my body. I was a cute girl, but my body was what gained all the guys attention.

My foster father and I began having sex, at first it was rape, but when he started buying me things, I was willing to open my legs for him. Around that time, I sunk into a deep depression and started to cut. When I was cutting my skin, I felt good. It was a feeling that no drugs or liquor could give you. When my foster mom realized I was cutting myself, she sent me to the crazy house and I stayed there for a year.

When I got out, I was assigned to a new foster house with new foster children. They were a really religious family. I went to church every Sunday, I attended Catholic school, was in bible study, choir, and all. I was doing ok until I met Nate. He was the first guy that I really fell in love with.

Because I was underage, I had to skip school or sneak out of the house to see him. After messing with Nate for two years, I became pregnant. To me, it was the happiest moment because we always talked about having a family.

The day I told him about the baby was the day he broke it off admitting that he couldn't deal with me anymore, because I wasn't worth losing his family. For two years, he would dodge his wife and kids to be with me, but all of a sudden they meant the world to him.

My whole pregnancy I sunk back into that deep depression. Once my foster parents got word of the baby, they isolated me. Since they were believers of

God, they did not believe in abortions, but they also didn't want the world to know that their sixteen-year-old daughter was pregnant out of wedlock.

The whole nine months I was stuck in the house. I was home schooled; I even attended church at home every Sunday. The day I gave birth to my daughter was the day I signed over my rights to my foster parents. I allowed them to raise her as their own. The day I returned home from the hospital was the day I took off in the middle of the night and never looked back.

To survive, I started sleeping with men for money. I no longer had the drug habit anymore, but I still used cutting to cope. One day while I was working the corner, a Rick Ross lookalike by the name of Bear approached me asking for the price of my services. Once we worked out a deal, I got in his car and he led me back to a hotel. I gave him the head that he requested, but he refused to pay me.

After allowing his homeboys to run multiple trains on me, he tied me up, and brought me to a warehouse.

The day Stacks came and recused me was the day I fell in love with him. Although I knew he had a pregnant girlfriend somewhere out there, I didn't care. There were days that I would get on my knees and pray that he would find her dead, so that we could move on with our lives.

When my prayers went unanswered, I was crushed. It was Nate all over again; he was pushing me away to be with his family. I let Nate go without a fight, but this time I vowed that Stacks would either be mines or no one else's. Cleaning up the blood off the kitchen floor, I went in the bathroom to take a nice, hot shower.

I was on the stove making dinner when I heard the front door open, a smile crept across my face hearing Stacks' footsteps.

"Why do you keep calling me?" he asked, getting in my face.

"I missed you that's all." I tried hugging him, but he pushed me off of him.

"How many times do I have to tell you there is nothing going on between us? Why can't you leave me alone?" he asked, he was so much taller than me so I had to look up at him as I spoke.

"It's not that easy."

"Tell me why! Why isn't it easy for you to leave a man that is in a happy relationship alone?"

"It's not easy because I love you!!!" I yelled, turning off the stove and running to my bedroom.

I flopped on my bed and began to cry hysterically. The urge to cut came over me again, but Stacks was here.

"I'm sorry if I led you on, but you knew the deal before I even allowed you to live in my house," he said, sitting on the edge of the bed.

"I know, but you can't control the heart."
I watched him as he put his head in his hands. His phone started to ring and I could tell by the ringtone that it was Lala. He ignored it; he just sat there with his head in hands, in deep thought. I didn't want to

stress him, but if he thought he was just going to dump me like last night's trash, he was wrong.

"What do you want from me?" he asked, breaking the silence.

"I want you."

"I already belong to someone, Amanda."

"I know, but I don't care."

"I'm not that type of guy; you're worth more than being someone's side bitch."

I knew he was right, but I still wanted him. I would rather share him than to not have him at all.

"I don't care," I said getting up and sitting in his lap. "I would rather have part of you than none of you. My heart will not be able to handle you not being here at all," I honestly stated.

I would rather be girlfriend number two than a distant memory.

"I'm sorry, Amanda, I can't. I love Lala too much to put her through that; she deserves to be treated with respect. You do too, but I'm not the one. It's not fair to string you along when my heart belongs to one woman."

He was rubbing my legs, looking me in the eyes, and telling me everything I didn't want to hear. I was agreeing to be the chick on the side and here he was turning my proposition down. I was done talking, my words weren't getting to him, so I decided to let my actions speak for me. I kissed him on the neck, licking that special spot that I recently discovered. His mouth was telling me he was done with me, but his dick was saying otherwise.

I sucked on his neck like a vacuum cleaner, determined to leave my mark. He was so into it that he didn't even realize what I was doing. He finally had enough of me teasing him; he lifted me and laid me flat on the bed. My pussy started doing cartwheels anticipating the feeling of his dick.

He tore my clothes off and flipped me over so that my ass was in the air. Rummaging through my nightstand he retrieved the box of condoms. I heard him open up the package and slide it on his dick. I held my breath waiting for him to enter him. He slapped my ass hard before roughly entering me causing me to cry out in pain.

"You better enjoy this dick because this is your last time getting it!" he yelled beating my pussy up as if he was Muhammad Ali in a boxing match.

"Do you hear me?" he asked as he pounded in and out of me.

"Yesssssssss daddy," I moaned reaching my third orgasm.

I wasn't leaving him alone until death does us apart.

Chapter 20
Stacks

I regretted the day I ever brought Amanda to my house. Part of this was my fault; I should have left her alone when I realized that she didn't have any information on Lala's disappearance. Now she was becoming a major pain in my ass. I knew fucking her didn't make the situation any better, but I had to get her to leave me alone some way. If she kept going over her boundaries, then I would be forced to kill her ass, and that was something I really didn't want to do.

I pulled up to the warehouse where they had Bear's brother waiting on me. Word on the street was that he'd been selling out on how Bear was able to get one over on me. I was about to do to his ass the same thing I was going to do to Bear as soon as I caught up with him. The sounds of someone being beaten echoed through the room. When I finally made it to where they were located, I could see Dixon tied to a chair receiving a beating from Ralph.

"What did I miss?" I asked putting on a clear suit to cover up my body; I wasn't trying to mess up my Armani fit.

"Nothing much boos, just warming him up or you," Ralph said stepping to the side.

"I have one question for you, if you answer it correctly, I will allow you to live despite the disrespect," I lied, either way I was going to kill him.

"Do you know where Bear is?" I asked picking up the weapon of my choice.

"Fuck you nigga," he replied, spitting blood on me.

"Fuck me?"

173

"Yes fuck you, like I fucked your bitch! The pussy was good, too! I'm thinking about digging her out her grave just to fuck her again," he laughed.

"Pull his pants down," I ordered, putting on a pair of gloves.

With one swift motion, I sliced his dick off.

"Ahhhhhh," he screamed, in agony.

"You want to rape women with this little ass dick of yours, now let me show you how it feels."

I took his dick and shoved it down his throat, he gagged throwing it up.
"Whats wrong, you can dish it, but you can't take it?" I taunted him shoving his face in his throw-up. I then took my knife and shoved it up his ass. I felt the bones in his ass crack with every thrust of my knife. When I was satisfied with the damage, I sliced his chest open and pulled out his heart.

"Send this to his mother," I said. "And call the cleanup crew and have them clean up this mess!" I shouted. Taking off the suit and the gloves, I left the warehouse and made my way home.

As soon as I went home, I headed to my man cave and decided to shower in there instead of the master bathroom. I wasn't ready to deal with Lala yet. In the shower, I couldn't help but shed a few tears for Donna, I failed her as a man and here I was doing the same with Lala.

While I was shaving, I noticed the hickey on my neck.

"Fuck!" I screamed, punching a hole in the wall.

How could I be so fucking dumb? There was no way in hell I was going to be able to hide this from Lala. Finishing up in the bathroom, I walked to the bar and rolled me a few blunts. Thank God I had a mini fridge stocked up with food in here, because I planned on hiding out in here for as long as possible.

Chilling on the leather sectional that furnished the room, I was smoking, drinking, and catching up on my sports when I heard a knock at the door.

"I didn't know you were here," Lala said walking towards me.

"Yeah, I was here just clearing my head," I said adjusting my body by laying the left side of my body on the couch.

"You had a long day?" she asked cuddling up under me.

"Something like that," I replied.

She grabbed the remote and changed the TV channel to LMN. I watched the movie with her until we fell asleep.

WHAM!

A slap to my face woke me up out of my sleep.

"What the fuck!" I roared.

"So, you were fucking that bitch?!" Lala shrieked, slapping me again.

"Lala, chill the fuck out yo' for real." I pushed her off me and got off the couch. She was right on my heels.

"You coming home with hickeys and shit, so are you fucking her, Anthony?"

"I'm not fucking anyone but you."

"So, explain why there is a hickey on your neck?" She had her hand propped on her hips waiting on my reply.

"Bear's brother burned me with a cigarette," I lied

"A fucking cigarette? Really? Do I look like I ride a fucking short yellow bus?!" She was furious, I could tell by the tears building up in her eyes.

I hated myself for what I was going to do, but I couldn't lose her.

"I swear to God, Lala, on everything I love. I confronted him on Bear's whereabouts and we got into an altercation."

"So, you're trying to tell me that Bear's brother used your neck as an ashtray?" she challenged.

"Yes, call Ralph if you don't believe me," I pleaded.

I dialed Ralph's number and handed her the phone and she walked out of the room to speak in private. I quickly grabbed my business phone and texted Ralph to put him up on game, deleting the text; I put the phone back on the counter and prayed that he got the text before he answered the phone.

After talking on the phone for almost an hour, Lala walked back into the room and threw the phone at me. She caught me off guard therefore I wasn't able to catch the phone. Looking down at my shattered phone, I feared the worst. My business phone beeped, it was a text from Ralph telling me he had me covered. I was happy my boy looked out for me.

Walking through the house in search of Lala, I found her sitting in her woman cave sipping wine and reading on her Kindle.

"Yo' what the fuck you are you doing?" I slapped the wine glass out of her hand and yoked her ass up.

"It's ok to have one glass of red wine once a week. It flushes out the toxins in your system and it also helps with the baby's mental development."

"How the fuck you know?"

"In case you forgot, I'm a fucking nurse! Unlike some people I would never intentionally try to hurt someone I loved," she rolled her eyes.

"Lala, stop acting like that, you know the truth."

"That doesn't mean I have to accept it."

"Shut up and come give your man kiss." I pulled her to me and began planting kisses all over her neck before passionately kissing her.

I laid her on the sofa, positioning my body on top of hers. Slipping my hands in her shorts, I pushed on her love button, causing an overflow of her juices to trickle down my hand staining the chair.

"Ohhhh," she let out a throaty moan, as she pushed my head deeper into her breast. I teased her nipples with the tip of my tongue, gently biting down on them. Kissing down her stomach, I used my tongue to play with her navel. The lower I went, the more my mouth watered, craving what she possessed between her legs. I ran my tongue over her freshly shaven pussy, the scent of her love drove me crazy, I couldn't resist, I had to taste it. Dipping my tongue in her pussy, I tested the temperature making sure it was hot and gushy, just the way I liked it.

I licked every inch of her pussy, capturing her clit in mouth, pulling and tugging on it, before sucking it until it become sensitive to touch. She began to squirm underneath me, so I used my arms to lock her in place.

"Stop pleasssssssssse," she begged me, trying to sit up and scoot away. The sensation she was feeling was unbearable. Ignoring her pleas, I sucked harder and harder on her clit. The way her legs were trembling it felt like a category five earthquake. Her breathing started to get heavy, as she laid there limp, trying to recuperate from the best head she'd ever received.

"Fuck me daddy," she muttered

"No, bad girls don't deserve dick." I gazed at her with lust filled eyes.

"I've been a good girl," she purred in a naughty voice that drove me crazy.

"Why you doubting your man?" I groaned, rubbing my dick up and down her pussy

"I'm sorry daddy, fuck me please!" she begged.

I filled her up with my dick, giving her a reward for promising to be a good girl for now own.

"Why you so tight?" I said. "You about to make me nut, see you being a bad girl again."

Which each thrust I felt myself sinking in her wetness. She arched her back, spreading her legs wider, letting me know that I was hitting her spot. She started to match my thrust, throwing the pussy at me. "That's right fuck daddy," I yowled, pushing her legs as far back as they could go. "Goddamn it!" I said, stroking faster and faster, feeling myself about to explode.

"On the count of ten, I want you to nut for daddy," I demanded

I silently counted in my head, by the time I reached five she was already creaming all over my dick.

"So, you don't know how to follow directions?" I asked flipping her over and roughly entering her from the back

"Oh, shit, Stacks! Fuuuuuuuuuuk," she called out in pure bliss.

Right before she was going to come, I pulled out.

"What the fuck!" she yelled, looking back at me.

"You want your nut, come ride this dick," I said, lying flat on my back.

She mounted me and rode me with so much force I thought she was going to tear my dick off.

"Ride this dick ma," I encouraged her, pulling her down to me by her hair for a kiss.

She started jumping on my dick uncontrollably, clenching her pussy muscles around my dick, all it took was a few more bounces and I was emptying my whole nut sack in her. She slowly grinded on my dick, throwing her head back in ecstasy. When she finally came, it felt like I was a part of the ice bucket challenge, except her juices were nice and warm.

She collapsed on my chest out of breath.

"I love you, Lala," I spoke, meaning every word.

"I love you, too, Anthony."

Chapter 21

Ralph

OJ Da Juiceman's *Make Tha Trap Say Aye* was bumping in the background in the trap as I sat in my office smoking blunt and counting money. A loud commotion in the other room reverted my attention from the massive amount of money I had in front of me. I had to have all of this money counted and packed before Stacks came and did his rounds.

I didn't trust anyone else around my money, so I opted to do it alone, unless Stacks was here to help me. Looking at the monitor, I saw a fight break out between two of my female workers. Punching in the code, I locked my office door, before going to see what was going on.

The scene before me looked like something you would see during a fight in high school. Everyone was just standing around hooting and hollering, each cheering a girl on.

"That's enough!" I yelled, breaking up the fight.

When I finally got Bebe to let go of Kandi's hair, I could see a gash on her forehead pouring out blood.

"J-Mack, take Bebe to the back," I ordered, one of my runners, as I took Kandi to the bathroom to get cleaned up.

"What the fuck happened?" I asked, wetting a rag and applying pressure to her wound.

"I'm not built for this," she said sobbing. "All I told her that it wasn't fair that she got to leave and go to the club while all of us had to work until the shipment was done. Then out of nowhere she just jumped on me and attacked me."

I examined her face and Bebe did a number on her. Kandi was so small and sexy compared to Bebe's beasty and ugly ass. Kandi was right she wasn't built for this life. She was a sweet, quiet girl that spoke proper, and dressed professionally to bag up dope. On the other hand, Bebe was as hood as they came. She was twenty-six with five kids, she was born in raised in the slums of Dade. She was making a grand every week only working three days a week and still was milking the government for every assistance they had to offer.

"All I wanted was to save up enough money to move to New York to attend NY Fashion University," she sniffled, wiping her eyes with the back of her hand.

"How much is your school?"

"It's twenty-thousand; I have ten thousand saved up. I would appreciate it if you would switch my days, so that I won't have to work with Bebe anymore," she sweetly said.

That's what I loved about her; she took this job very seriously. She treated it as if she was working a 9-5."

"I think it would be best if I just let you go, you're not about this life."

"But I need the money," she cried.

"I got you." I left her standing in the bathroom and went back to my office to retrieve money.

"Here you go, this should cover your school and expenses," I said, handing her a duffle bag with fifty-grand in it.

"Thank you so much," she beamed, hugging me

"No, problem ma. I don't want to see you in no place like this no more. Only bitches like Bebe are limited to this type of work, but you, you have drive, dedication, and potential."

"Thank you, I appreciate that."

"Anytime ma, let me walk you to your car. The pit-bull might still be loose," I said laughing.

Making sure she was secured in her car, I gave her my number and told her to call me anytime.

I sent Bebe home for the day with a warning, and went back to counting money. Halfway through, my phone beeped letting me know that I had a text message.

It was from my daughter confirming our dinner and a movie date tonight. I responded to her letting her know that I would be there at 6pm on the dot.

Looking at my watch, I had two hours left until 6. I put a little more pep in my step and got down to finishing up counting this money. When I was done, I packed Stacks' cut of the money and put it in the safe for him. Saying my goodbyes; I made my way home then I would take my princess out on a date.

Arriving to my house, I opened my attic door to deposit my money in my safe. Looking at the time, I noticed that it was already 5:30. I went to take a quick shower and got dressed. Stopping at a flower shop, I bought my daughter some yellow daisies. At an early age, I was training her on how a man should treat her. I didn't want her growing up not knowing her worth. There were too many lost females falling victim to no good ass niggas and I would be damned if mine was one of them.

Parking my car, I got out and knocked on the door.

"She's mad," Laurie said, when she opened the door. "Riley daddy is here."

My baby girl came to the door looking so cute in her pink and purple dress, her hair was neatly braided with clear beads at the end of them. She sported the gold nameplate jewelry set I bought her.

"You're late, Daddy!" she said, pouting her lips.

"I know baby, I'm sorry, I got a little caught up at work," I said picking her up. "Look what daddy got you." I handed her the flowers and she brought them up to her nose to smell them.

"Thank you, Daddy," she smiled.

"When are you bringing her home?" Laurie asked.

"Sunday night."

"Ok," she replied giving me Riley's overnight bag. "Have fun with Daddy," she said to our daughter giving her a kiss.

"I will, Mommy, and can you put these in water for me, please?" she politely asked her mother, handing her the flowers.

"Okay baby, see you later."

"Later, Mommy."

"Daddy, if we miss the movie I am going to be upset," she said as I strapped her in the backseat.

"We won't miss it, I promise," I assured her.

Following the movie, I took her to Chili's for dinner. During dinner, we had small talk about school, Christmas, and her birthday. She even lectured me on the importance of me getting married, so that I could give her a baby sister. A voice caught my attention. Looking to my left, I spotted Lisa and a guy being seated two tables away from us. I felt myself boil with anger, she wasn't my girl, but that didn't stop me from getting jealous.

"Daddy, why do you keep looking at her?" Riley asked.

"No, reason, are you ready to go?"

"Yes. Daddy, can we go get ice cream on the beach?"

"It's getting kind of late, Ry."

"Pleeeeeeeease," she begged, batting her long, thick eyelashes.

"Okay."

I paid the bill, and as we were leaving the restaurant, we bumped right into Lisa.

"Hey, Ralph," she greeted and gave me a hug.

"Why are you playing these games?" I whispered in her ear, brushing my lips across her earlobe.

"Hey cutie," she smiled down at Riley.

"Hi, my name is Riley. What's your name?"

"Lisa. Riley is a very pretty name for a perfect little girl."

I stood back with a smile on my face as I watched them interact with each other.

"Would you like to come join daddy and me for ice-cream?" Riley asked in her baby doll voice.

"I'm kind of busy, but I'll see," she hesitated while answering.

"Lose that nigga, and meet us down at Jack's Ice Cream Shack. Don't make me have to come back out here and get you," I said low enough, for only her to hear me.

We were chilling on the beach, feet in the water, eating ice cream, when Lisa finally decided to join us.

"Hey, Lisa!" Riley bounced up and down.

"Hey, cutie pie," Lisa giggled.

Lisa removed her shoes and sat next to me.

"Are you happy you ruined my date?"

"That nigga was a lame if you ask me," I told her straight up.

"How you figure?"

"He let you out of his sight. He fucked up and now I'm about to luck up," I confidently stated.

"What makes you so sure?"

"Because I am that nigga," I smiled.

We chilled at the beach a little while longer. I was able to convince Lisa to come back to the house with the help of Riley. The beauty of kids. When we finally got home, Riley was knocked out. I let Lisa in and carried Ry to her room. Laying her in her bed, I kissed her goodnight and made sure her Frozen DVD was on replay.

"Nice spot," Lisa complimented.

"Yeah, I try," I said. "Make yourself at home."

I pulled out a pound of Jimmie Dean Kush and started rolling me a blunt.

"You smoke?" I asked firing up the blunt.

"Naw," She declined.

"Why? You can't hang?"

"I can hang. I just rather have a clear head while dealing with you."

"What is that supposed to mean?"

"I'm not trying to make any under the influence choices."

"Why not? YOLO! Let's turn up. Plus an under the influence mind tells the truth." I grabbed a bottle of Remy and a deck of cards.

"You know how to play spades?" I asked taking a seat at the dining room table.

"Do I? I'm the queen baby," she said joining me at the table. "I don't play for free though."

"I have something in mind," I licked my lips.

"What?"

"We play for clothes. Every time we play a game, the loser has to take off a piece of clothing. At the end, whoever has on the least amount of clothing has to give the other person a lap dance."

"Well, I hope you know how to twerk then," she said shuffling the deck of cards.

Enjoying each other's company, we smoked, drank, and played cards. At the end of the game, I was down to my boxers while the only piece of clothing Lala had to remove was her jeans.

"Looks like I win," she smirked.

"Aight then, come enjoy the show," I said leading her to my bedroom. I dimmed the lights and hit play button on the stereo. Chris Brown's *Strip* started to play, and I tried my best to do just that.

I was high as fuck and borderline drunk. I had no issue making a fool of myself. I sat on her lap and grinded my dick into her. She opened her legs wider, and I could see the seat of her crotch was moist. When I ran out of dance moves, I sat her on my back and did one-handed push-ups. I could tell she was getting turned on by the way she was rubbing on my back muscles.

The song ended, so I picked her up, carried her to my bed, and laid her down. I climbed in bed with her and turned on the TV. I was watching, *Storage Wars* when I felt a pair of hands slip in my boxers.

"Stop," I said pulling her hand out of my drawers.

"Why?" she whined.

"Because you're not ready yet."

"Yes, I am."

"Naw Ma, that's just the weed talking," I explained.

"What happened to an under the influence mind tells the truth?" she asked.

"Yeah, you're right, and right now you are letting me know you want me sexually. I want you to want me emotionally as well. I'm not trying to fuck. I want something real," I said laying it all on the line.

"I hear you."

"You hear me, but do you understand me?" I asked.

"Yes!"

"When you finally stop playing and you're mine, I'm going to bless you with the best dick you ever had," I smiled pulling her close to me.

We laid in silence before I heard her lightly snoring. I got up to make sure the alarm was on, checked on Ry, and came back to bed.

Chapter 22
Bear

I was fucked up in the head over the events that took place. I swear I had all my confidence in that bitch Tasha, but she fucked up and got herself killed. I was trying to get in touch with Pablo and haven't been able to. I kept thinking he sold me out to Stacks to avoid getting caught, either way I was pissed. I was too paranoid to live in Dubai anymore, so I caught a flight back home to Flint and was crashing with my mom.

"Are you okay, Mom?" I asked.

Recently, she received a box with my brother's heart in it saying,

Your heartless sons don't deserve to live, one down, one more to go.

Since my mother only had two sons, and I was perfectly fine, it had to be Dixon.

"Who would do this to my baby, Kenneth?" she sobbed.

"I don't know, Mom, but when I find out, I'm going to handle it," I consoled her while shedding a tear.

A part of me believed Stacks had something to do with my brother being butchered. We couldn't give my brother a proper burial because we had no idea where his body was located. It was only a matter of time before I went back up to Miami and ended this shit once and for all. I had plans on emptying two clips of bullets in his ass since he wanted to be 50-Cent and shit.

With Pablo disappearing on me, my money started to dry up. I was down to my last thirty-thousand, and I knew that wasn't going to last very long. I really had to sit down and think of a perfect plan. If everything went my way, I could carry out my original plan on robbing and killing Stacks. Everything had to be planned out to perfection. I had to have the right man on my team and an inside leak.

"Ma, I'll be back," I said, grabbing her keys and making my way to the turf of the enemy. Back when Stacks and I were hustling back in Flint, we stepped on a lot of toes and made a lot of enemies. Now, I needed these enemies to help me take out my biggest one, Stacks.

Parking the car, I made my way to the Arcade where a majority of Alan's crew was located. Alan and Stacks held a lot of animosity towards each other, especially since I was able to convince Stacks that it was Alan and his crew who had something to do with Donna's death. Before Stack's left for Miami, these streets turned into a major war zone.

"What the fuck you doing down here nigga?" Nico asked pulling his gun out on me and aiming towards my head. I had about thirty seconds to tell his ass something good or my brain matter would paint the ground. Nico was Alan's right-hand man and in order for me to get to him, I had to get through this first.

"I have information that could help Alan get up with Stacks," I said looking in his eyes.

"So, let me get this right," he laughed. "You want to help us take down your homeboy?"

"Yes! That nigga violated in the worst way. He killed my girl and my brother, and I want his ass to pay in blood."

"You better tell me something good before I shoot your ass right now."

"Stacks was the one who killed Alan's cousin," I lied.

I was the one who convinced him into confessing he had something to do with Donna's murder and killed him before he could reveal my secret.

"Follow me," Nico said, lowering his gun.

We entered the backroom of the arcade that led to his office.

"What the fuck you doing bringing trash in my office," Alan said, staring at me with cold eyes.

"Yo', A, he got some information that is very beneficial to us," Nico spoke.

"Speak then nigga."

"I can help you take down that nigga Stacks."

"What makes you think I need your help? Stacks is no longer in Flint, so he ain't fucking with my cash flow."

"Stacks killed Pewee," I blurted out, to catch his attention. His eyes turned a shade of red and I could see the anger written in them.

"How do you know?" he inquired.

"I was there," I said. "Plus taking down Stacks will come with a major payout. His father is the head of Columbia's cartel, once he steps down, he will be passing the throne down to Stacks. You think there's money down here? Man this is lunch money to the numbers Stacks is making in Miami."

"How do I know you're not bullshitting?" he asked.

"Man, I put this on my mother."

"Okay. Fine. Rico send someone to Bear's house to pick up his mother. Any false move and I'm killing her dead," he spit.

My heart sunk down to the pit of my stomach. I was confident that we would be able to take down Stacks, but I didn't want my mother a part of this.

"You're dismissed. I'll get up with you later," he said.

Plan one was live in effect, now it was time to set plan two in motion. Dressed in all black, I sat across the street from my victim's house waiting for them to turn all the lights out. When the kitchen light finally went off, and I was sure everyone in the house was fast asleep, I crept across the street and picked the lock to the front door allowing myself entrance into the house.

Entering the bedroom, my prey was sleeping peacefully. I walked over to Stacks' grandpa and slit his throat. I then walked over to his grandma and did the same. I sliced both of their chests open, removing their hearts. I took the note out of my pocket that read,

Come catch this heartless motherfucker if you can.

I taped it to Stacks' grandpa's forehead and left the crime scene. You take one of mine; I take two of yours. I removed my gloves and the clothing I was wearing. I put them in a plastic bag and threw them in the back of my trunk. I pulled the pre-rolled blunt out of my ashtray and fired it up. Revenge was so close. I could feel it.

Chapter 23

Lala

Standing in the mirror, my insecurities were on full display. Stacks was due to come home from his business trip with Carla, and I was feeling some type of way. Even though he assured me plenty of times there was nothing going on between them and it was just business, I knew otherwise. The way she looked at him was the way you look at someone you love. I was very much familiar with that look. It was the same look I woke up to every morning.

I was now five months pregnant and barely showing. I carried my baby in my thighs. My already fat ass was now more plump and wide. My breast grew a cup size, and my hair was longer and thicker. My pregnancy gave me this glow that made my skin rich. All in all I was a very beautiful woman, inside and out. There was no reason for me to feel insecure, but when Stacks started to ignore my calls, come home late, and have hickies all over his neck, I couldn't help but to feel this way.

I knew that day when he came home something wasn't right. He never came home without looking for me first. The part that confused me was when he smelt like a fresh bar of soap. That was real suspect. Why would he shower in his man cave instead of the master bedroom? I wanted so badly to stay mad at him, but whenever I tried to put up a fight to get my point across, he used his dick to get me back in check.

Watching the clock, it was now seven pm. His flight was scheduled to be here at five pm and he still hadn't shown up yet, nor did he give me a courtesy call to let me know he landed safely. When we spoke yesterday, I offered to come pick him up from the airport, but he declined stating he would have to make a few runs. Picking up the phone, I called the only person that knew the exact words to tell me to make me feel better.

"Hello," Lisa cheered.

"Somebody's in a good mood."

"I sure am," she beamed.

"I take it that your date with Max went great."

"Not necessarily," she said. "Enough about me. What's wrong?"

"Why do you do that?" I asked.

"Do what?"

"Worry about me more than yourself? You always push your problems to the side for mine."

"Because that's what best bitches do!" she laughed. "But for real, what's wrong?"

"I don't feel like he appreciates me anymore," I sighed.

"This is how you give that nigga a dose of act right. Are you listening?"

"You so silly. Yes, I'm listening."

"Get real cute. I mean put on your sexiest outfit, curl your hair, paint your toes, and make sure your makeup is nothing less than flawless. When you hear him come through the door, sashay your ass past him without uttering a word, get in your car, and come over here for a movie night," she laughed.

"You want me to get dressed up to come to your house?"

"Yes, but he won't know that. Go get ready, and I will see you when you get here!" She hung up.

Standing in my walk-in closet, I searched for something to wear. After thirty minutes of going through racks of clothing, I decided on my little black freakum dress from Chanel. Laying my clothes on the bed, I went in the bathroom to handle my hygiene.

Drying my body off, I applied the lavender body oil to every inch of my body before putting on my sheer lace black thong and bra set. Spraying my body with the lavender body mist, I sat at my vanity and applied my makeup.

Satisfied with how my make-up turned out, I added my MAC ruby red lipstick, coating it with my shimmer gloss. It gave my lips the full plump effect. Curling my hair, I pinned it up so my curls would fall down like waterfalls. I clasped my thirty-three carat, platinum diamond necklace around my neck, putting the matching earrings in my ears, and bracelet on my wrist.

Pulling the dress over my body, I slipped my feet into my black wedges. I grabbed my black clutch and did a final look through. Spinning in the mirror, I was looking fierce! I grabbed my Burberry perfume, Stacks' favorite scent on me, and sprayed it all over. When I was done, I went downstairs and took a seat on the couch and waited for Stacks to come home.

It was nine o'clock when he finally pulled up. I walked from the elevator to make it seem like I was just coming down. As he was walking in, I tried to walk past him, but he grabbed me by the arm, and pulled me into a hug.

"Where are you going with that little ass dress at this time of night?" he asked.

I could smell the liquor on his breath and the weed on his clothes.

"I'm going out to celebrate a co-worker's birthday."

"You never told me about it."

"When are you ever home for me to tell you anything?" I snapped.

"Well, you ain't going," he said, with his hand under my dress rubbing my ass cheeks. "Especially not with them little ass drawers on."

"Check the bitch that was giving you hickeys on your neck," I said breaking his embrace. I walked away from him putting an extra switch in my ass.

My phone rang back to back the whole drive to Lisa's house. Hitting the clicker on my key, I decided to park in her garage knowing this would be Stacks' first place to look for me.

"You finally made it," Lisa said. "Does that mean he's just now getting in, or did you slip up and give that nigga some ass?"

"I did not give him any. If I did, I wouldn't be here right now," I answered, taking off my dress and shoes. "What you got to eat in here?"

"Fat ass always thinking about food. The pizza should be here soon."

My phone started ringing again, after ringing off the hook for about twenty minutes a text from Stacks beeped through.

Don't make me come looking for you!!!

Lisa grabbed the phone and turned it off. We sat and enjoyed each other's company. It had been a while since we had one of these chill out days, and I was glad I came. The pizza came. We ate and talked about her new love interest, Ralph.

"You expecting a guest?" I asked noticing headlights beaming through the window.

"No," she said, walking to the window. "Oh shit, Stacks is here go upstairs."

I picked up all of my belongings and ran into Lisa's room. I left the door cracked a little, so I could eavesdrop on their conversation.

"Is Lala here?" I heard Stacks ask as soon as she opened the door.

"No, should she be here?"

"Man." He let out a breath of frustration. "Can you try calling her for me?"

Lisa dialed my number and it went straight to voicemail.

"So, you tryna tell me Lala is missing again?" Lisa yelled.

"No, she said she as going out with co-workers."

"Okay, so why are you here?"

"You think she's fucking around on me?"

"Are you fucking serious! She is pregnant. Lala has way more class than that."

"Yeah, I bet, not with that little ass dress she had on," he said. "Well, if you see her, tell her bring her ass home ASAP!"

"Whatever," Lisa replied, closing the door.

Chapter 23

Stacks

I tried tracking Lala's iPhone, but was coming up with no location because she turned her phone off. I swear when she came home I was going to fuck her ass up on sight. Using my key to Amanda's apartment, I went in to have a few words with her. I was going to shake some sense into her, or she was going to come up missing.

I still had the phone to my ear attempting to reach Lala as I walked inside the house. Hearing her voicemail again enraged me. I stuffed the phone in my pocket and headed toward the kitchen where I heard pots and pans being shuffled around.

Amanda's back was towards me when I ran up on her and snatched her up by the neck.

"What the fuck!" she screamed.

"You fucked up my home bitch! All I did was try to be nice to your dumb ass, but you had to get sprung off the dick and go to acting crazy!"

"What the fuck are you talking about?"

"The fucking hickey? Amanda you did that shit on purpose. What did you think you were going to get out of this?" I scoffed.

"I just want you all to myself," she admitted.

I tightened the grip I had around her neck as I spoke.

"Ungrateful ass bitch! I bought you this house, got you a car, and gave you more than enough money to live your life. I told you upfront that I wasn't leaving her for you. What you thought I was joking?"

I let go of her throat and threw her on the floor. She was gasping for air, sucking in huge amounts of it.

"So, I never meant anything to you?" she cried.

"NOTHING!" I yelled. "Leave me the fuck alone! Don't call me, don't text me, just delete me out your fucking memory bank, or else."

"Or else what?" she challenged.

"I'll kill your ass! That's what!"

I took her key off my key chain and threw it at her ass, turned around, and walked out of the house.

It was midnight when I made it home, and there was no sign of Lala. I walked through the house looking in every room, praying she would be here, but was disappointed. All her things were still in the closet, so she had to come back home eventually.

Lighting a blunt, I went out on the balcony to ease my mind. The sound of the water crashing against the shore relaxed me. I sat outside until about two am before I decided to call it a night.

The next morning, I woke up love sick. Lala still hadn't made it home. A part of me knew she was okay since Lisa didn't call me asking for her. I felt like my world was turning upside down. I wished for a time machine, so I could go back in time and correct all my wrongs.

If she left me, I couldn't blame her. I became the same nigga I worked so hard to steal her from. I had to get my act together and quick before I pushed her into the arms of another man.

I had to meet up with Carla to talk about expanding. I was talking Ralph along with me because I was not trying to be anywhere alone with that girl. I already fucked up, and I wasn't trying the whole 'I was in any deeper than I thought'.

My stomach started to sing to me, so I made myself some breakfast. Sitting down to eat, I tried calling Lala again, and her phone was finally ringing, she just wasn't answering her calls. I logged into my MacBook Pro to track her iPhone and just as I suspected she was at Lisa's house.

I was going to allow her to chill out over there and cool down for a bit, but I planned on dragging her ass home if she thought she was going to spend another night away from me.

*****

Business was going very well, and I was happy at how professional Carla was keeping it. I was kind of skeptical about the merge since she was running things on the behalf of her family, but she was proving me wrong. I was happy when I got home, and Lala's car was parked in the driveway.

I ran to the door and opened it up only to find packed bags by the door.

"Lala, can you explain this shit to me?" I said.

"I'll let your bitch explain it for you." She hit play on her phone, and my conversation with Amanda was being played. I must have forgotten to hang up the phone, and everything was recorded on her voicemail.

"Lala, baby I'm sorry."

"No, I'm sorry! Sorry for thinking you were any different than James." She took the ring off her finger and handed it to me. I refused to take it, so she sat it on the coffee table.

"So, it's that easy for you to walk away from me, after everything we've been through you not gonna even try to work it out with a nigga?"

"No, because you lied! You lied to me twice. I asked you did you fuck her, and you told me no. Then you lied about the hickey. Not to mention you bought her a fucking house and car. You were over there giving her the main bitch treatment," she laughed.

"It was an accident."

"So you slipped, fell, and landed dick first in her pussy? Is that what you're telling me?"

I felt myself losing this battle. I couldn't allow her to walk out this door without hearing me out first. I wrapped my arms around her and held her tight.

'No one else comes close to you, no one makes me feel the way you do, you're so special to me girl, and you'll always be eternally, every time I hold you near, you always say the words I love to hear, girl with just a touch, you can do so much, no one else comes close.'

I sang the lyrics to Joe's *No One Else Comes Close* song with so much passion in her ear. I felt her tears stain my neck as I continued to sing to her. I had to make her feel that she meant the world to me. Even though I fucked up, I deserved to have her in my life. I was too selfish to allow her to leave me and possibly find the next nigga to be with.

"Anthony, I can't do this anymore. I allowed myself to go through this with James and I vowed never to put myself in that predicament again. If I take you back, you're going to think it's okay to sing a song or stick your dick in me, and all will be forgiven. Well, that's not how it works, Stacks, you can't manipulate my feelings anymore," she sobbed.

"Lala, are you ready?" Lisa asked walking through the door.

"Yes, these are my bags. I'll wait for you in the car," she said pulling away from me and walking away.

"Lisa, talk some sense into ya' girl," I begged.

"I'll try, but you fucked up!"

"I know, just help me make it right."

"I got you kid, just don't run up in anymore pussy, let her know you're serious about putting in the effort to make it work."

"Good looking out."

I walked her to the door and watched the love of my life drive away. This big house felt so empty. Taking the elevator to my man cave, I went to the bar, grabbed me a bottle, and started to drink my pain away. I smoked and drank until I saw stars. Resting my head on the couch, I prayed that God would send my baby back to me.

Chapter 24

Ashley

"He did what?" I half listened to Amanda.

"Came to the house and choked me up over that bitch?"

"Damn, what did you do?"

"I gave him a hickey on purpose," she smiled. "And I guess she found out."

"He'll be back, they always do. Trust me I know."

I couldn't count the amount of times James used to choke, hit, bite, or slap me for fucking with Lala, but he never could stay away. Niggas could never get enough of their side bitch.

"So, what are you going to do now?" I asked.

"I'ma let him cool off."

"I hear you," I said getting up and wobbling towards the bathroom.

I was eight months pregnant and bigger than a house. I was prepared to have this little boy any day now. I still wasn't able to get in contact with Pablo. Even Bear had changed his number on me. It was just my child and I in this world. That was fine by me because I planned on using Amanda as my puppet and if she did everything I told her, my baby wasn't going to be the only one fatherless.

"This baby got me peeing every five minutes," I said taking a seat on the barstool.

"Where is your baby daddy?" Amanda asked.

"Out of town."

"Y'all must not live together."

"Why you say that?" I smacked my lips.

"I don't see anything that indicates a man lives here," she said looking around my apartment.

"Who said he lives here?" I snapped.

"Sorry, I just assumed…"

"Well, stop assuming shit!"

"Okay, whatever. You ready to go to the mall, so I can spoil my god baby or what?"

I rolled my eyes at her. I didn't know why hoes was so hard up for friends. All I did was listen to her vent once, and she thought we were the best of friends.

"With what money, I ain't seen your broke ass work a day since I've met you."

"I got this," she said waving Stacks' black card in the air.

"How did you get that?"

"Don't worry about it. You coming or what?"

"Hell, fuck yeah I'm coming!"

I had to find a way to get the black card. I was real good with the credit card scheme and if I could get over on a rich nigga like Stacks, I'd be straight.

Chapter 25

Lisa

I was walking around the house putting the final touches on my outfit for my first date with Ralph. At first, I was against dating. The only reason I was on a date with Max was because he was one of my sponsors. Since the whole bullshit with Bear and the accident, I decided to resume stripping, that was my way with coping with everything.

"If you want me to stay, I'll stay," I said noticing Lala moping.

"No, you go have fun. I'll be okay."

"You sure?"

"Yes, go have fun."

With her permission, I finished getting ready and left.

I met Ralph at Bistro 25. For a first date, he had great taste, and I was really impressed. Entering the restaurant, I felt all eyes on me. I bet they were trying to calculate how much the diamonds cost that I had around my neck.

"You look nice." Ralph stood, pulling out my chair.

"Thank you and you look nice yourself."

I swear this shit felt like déjà vu. Here I was on a date again with another one of Stacks' friends.

"How's Lala?" he asked.

"She's not too good. I'm not going to lie, all she does is mope and cry."

"Damn, that's fucked up."

I noticed him pick up the phone and send a text.

"Don't be texting your bitches while you out with me!" I fussed.

"What's up with the jealousy though?"

Before I could reply, the waiter came over to take our orders. I ordered the Parmesan crusted chicken, and he decided to go with the sirloin steak.

Taking a sip of my wine, I felt something that I haven't felt in months, butterflies. This guy was winning me over just from conversation alone. He was so educated and intellectual. If you didn't know, you wouldn't have guessed he sold drugs for a living. A hood nigga with book smarts was a perfect combination. Paying for our meal, he waited for the valet to bring my car around then asked me to follow him to his house.

My nerves were fucking with me. I couldn't even grip the steering wheel right because my palms were damp. Noticing that I was still sitting in my car, Ralph came over and tapped on the passenger's window. I unlocked the door, and he got in.

"So, you not coming in?" he asked. "What you scared of?"

"I just don't want to let my guard down only to get hurt."

"I'm not saying I'm perfect, but I'm willing to be perfected. Just give me a chance ma, rock with a nigga."

I sat and thought about the worst thing that could possibly happen. I was getting older, not younger, and it was time that I settled down.

"What are the plans for the rest of the night?" I asked.

"If you stop being scared and come inside, then you'll see."

He got out the car and walked over to the driver's side. Lifting me out of my seat, he hit the lock on my alarm and locked the door. He put me down when we got inside.

"Let's play a game," he said.

"You like to play a lot of games."

"What can I say, I'm a playful person."

"What game are we playing?"

"It's a treasure hunt game. There are clues all around the house that will lead you to where 'X' marks the spot," he smiled.

"Okay, where do I start?"

"Your first clue is in the kitchen, taped on the microwave."

Going inside the kitchen, I read the note that was attached to the microwave. On the front was the word 'will' and on the back was the location to where I would find the next clue. I walked around the house determined to solve this treasure hunt game. I hated to admit it, but I was actually enjoying myself. This was different. I never had a guy go through extreme measures for me.

The fourth word was 'my'. The back of the card directed me back to the living room where Ralph was sitting on the couch with the next clue taped to his mouth. The front of the note said that I would have to kiss him before reading the last clue. Leaning down, I planted a soft kiss on his lips, and then tore the note open.

'Girl' was the final word. I flipped the card over and saw a bunch of question marks. It took a moment for it to register in my head, but when it did I punched him in the shoulder.

"You didn't answer the question," he laughed.

"Where is the 'X'? I want my prize." I playfully rolled my eyes.

"Answer me first. My games, my rules."

"Yes."

"Yes what?"

"Yes, I'll be your girl."

"Here," he said handing me a box.

Tearing open the box, I stared at the most beautiful purple diamond bracelet ever. Engraved in it were the words:

Forever Ralph's girl.

"You like it?" he asked, clasping the bracelet around my wrist.

"I love it!"

I pushed him down on the couch and straddled him. I licked his neck softly, biting it, and then sucking it gently. I could hear his breathing become shallow when I started to slow grind on him to the beat that played in my head. I grabbed him by the head and started to kiss his lips, pulling on his bottom lip.

"Damn Ma, keep teasing me and I'ma flip yo ass over on this couch and put it on ya."

"Maybe that's what I want."

He got up off the couch with me still in his arms and brought me to the bedroom, laying me down his bed. Gently he peeled off my clothing, and he just stood there looking at me, admiring the sexiest body he probably had ever seen.

He turned me around, smacked my ass, and watched it jiggle. I made each of my ass cheeks bounce and jiggle as he watched in amazement. Spreading my cheeks apart, he started licking me from ass crack down to my pussy. The sensation I was feeling drove me crazy. I felt his wet, warm tongue enter my ass, and I swear I saw the gates of heaven open up.

After I came from him eating my ass, he went down to pay my pussy some attention. I was so wet that he had to swallow all my juices before he could reach my clit. I tried to crawl away from those lethal lips. I couldn't take what he was doing to me.

"Why you running?" he asked, wrapping his strong arms around my waist, holding me in place. Taking me by my now swollen pearl in his mouth, he sucked until I was speaking in tongues. He slapped my ass. The stinging sensation brought me to another orgasm.

I heard a drawer open and the opening of a package. When he was satisfied with the security of his dick, he took it and gently slid it in my hole. The sloshing sounds from him thrusting in and out of my slippery mound took over the room.

"Fuck me!" I moaned, throwing my head back.

"Like this?" he asked, pounding in and out with me with so much force I thought he was going to send me flying through the wall.

I held on to the headboard for dear life as he took me on a crazy orgasmic ride. The orgasms started hitting me back to back. He reached over and grabbed my clit, twirling it between his thumb and pointer finger. I collapsed on the bed, but he wasn't done with me yet. He flipped me over, threw both my legs over his shoulders and continued to give me those long death strokes. It was only thirty minutes into our love making session, and I was already gone off the "D". Making sure I was fully satisfied sexually, he then released his seeds into the condom and fell on top of me.

"Damn you got them sugar walls," he panted, trying to regulate his breathing.

I just laid there in silence. He fucked all the words out of me and now I was a mute. Laughing, he got up and went to the bathroom to flush the condom. I heard the water running, and then he returned with a warm washcloth. He spread my lips and kissed my pussy before washing me up.

Chapter 23

Lala

Life without Stacks really sucked. It had been a month since we'd really talked or seen each other. He would drop by and leave me money and groceries. Today I was six months, and I had a doctor's appointment. I was hoping that he/she would be in a position where I could finally find out the sex.

I was just leaving the yoga studio and Stacks was supposed to meet up with me at the doctor's office at four pm and it was now two. Grabbing my container of jerk chicken and shrimp, I hit the alarm on my car and made my way inside the house. Lisa and Ralph really had been kicking it this past month, so she was barely home. I wasn't mad at her though because she really did deserve someone after the damage Bear did to her heart.

"Where you go with them little ass shorts on?" Stacks' voice frightened me, causing me to drop my bag of food. He bent down, picked up the bag, and sat it on the coffee table. He then slipped his hands in my shorts, feeling to see what type of panties I had on. When he finished, I retrieved my food and went to go sit in the kitchen to eat. Before I could get the fork filled with cheesy pasta in my mouth, he was right on my heels questioning me again.

"I know you heard me ask you a question." He sat across from me, taking the fork out of my hand and shoving it in his mouth.

"This not too spicy for the baby?" he asked, before shoving another fork full of my food in his mouth.

"No." I grabbed the fork from him and started eating my food. He got up and went to refrigerator to get me a bottled water, taking the coke that I originally bought to drink.

"Where were you?" he asked again.

"Prenatal yoga."

"Why you had on them little ass shorts?"

"I had to dress comfortably."

"You could have worn some yoga pants. Hell ain't that what you supposed to wear while doing yoga?"

"You wear whatever makes you comfortable, and these shorts do, now leave me alone so I can eat." I was beyond irritated with his ass at this point that I lost my appetite.

"I'm just saying. You walking around with your ass jiggling and shit, that's not a good look. Acting like you ain't got no man or a baby in your stomach."

"I don't have a man."

"Yeah, whatever. Hurry up before you make us late."

"You were supposed to meet me at the doctor's office anyway and how in the hell did you get in this house?" I asked not remembering seeing his car in the driveway.

"Ralph dropped me off on his way to pick up Lisa."

I left him at the table eating the rest of my food and went to take a shower. Pinning my hair up then wrapping it, I got in the tub and began cleansing my body. As soon as I was done, I got out, dried my body and walked into the guest bedroom that I'd been staying in for the past month.

"Can you get out so I can get dressed?" I asked Stacks, who was sitting on the edge of my bed with a bottle of lotion in his hands.

"You don't have anything I haven't seen."

"So, but still, I..."

"Shut up and come here!" he yelled, cutting me off.

I slowly walked over to the bed. He pushed me down and began rubbing my naked body down with the lotion. He paid extra attention to my sensitive areas, making me squirm. When he started rubbing on my pussy, I spread my legs wide giving him more access. He closed my legs shut and started laughing.

"Why are you opening up your legs to me if I ain't your nigga?" he asked and stood up. "Hurry up before we're late." He walked out the room leaving me on the bed hot, wet, and horny.

"You look sexy as fuck," Stacks complimented me.

My hair was parted down the middle, bone straight. I was wearing a soft pink DKNY dress, paired with the matching sandals. I made sure I sprayed his favorite Burberry perfume on my body.

"Thanks."

I threw him the keys to my car, set the alarm, and got in the passenger's seat. The drive to the doctor's office was silent, except for Usher and Chris Brown singing about their *New Flame.* When we finally got there, I signed in and we waited in the waiting room to be called.

"Lala Williams," the young blond nurse called my name out.

She handed me a cup to pee in, checked my weight, blood pressure, and sent me to room three to wait on my doctor.

"How are you feeling today?" the doctor asked as she came in and took a seat in the chair that was next to the bed.

"I'm feeling great, just ready to see what we're having."

"Okay, then, let's get started."

She poured the warm, blue gel on my belly, and then started to search for my pumpkin.

"Legs are wide open today," she said snapping pictures of the baby.

I adjusted my eyes to the monitor trying to get a better look at the screen. She typed in the words, 'Daddy's little girl'.

"Time to buy some more guns," Stacks said after reading the words off the screen.

"Everything looks good. Just try to ease up a bit because your blood pressure is a little high right now. I want to see you back here in two weeks just to check your blood pressure, okay?"

"Okay."

"Megan will set your appointment for you. Congratulations on the little princess." She wiped the gel off my tummy then left the room.

"You ready to go shopping now?" Stacks asked as soon as we got in the car.

"Sure."

"So, when are you planning on coming home? You got me fucked up if you think my baby is going to be living in a separate house from me."

I didn't respond. I just cranked the volume to K. Michelle's *Can't Raise A Man.*

We ripped and ran through the mall. I went totally crazy. I grabbed any and everything I saw without checking the price tags. Lil mama put a five thousand dollar dent in daddy's pocket, and she wasn't even done yet.

"Damn Lala was it necessary to buy all this stuff?" he asked carrying the bags with the help of two security guards.

"Yes, she's a girl. She needs a lot of cute things to wear." I smiled.

Stopping at Steak-N'-Shake, we grabbed dinner and headed home. I went in the baby's nursery and put some of her things in the closet. I also called up the decorator I found online to let her know the theme I wanted for the baby's room.

Once I was done, I went to search for Stacks so he could take me back to Lisa's house. He told me he didn't want to live in a separate house from his baby. However the baby wasn't born yet. I found him lying in the bed stripped down to his boxers, wife beater, and socks.

"I'm ready to go, can you take me home now?"

"This is home," he replied.

"Well, can you hand me my keys, so I can head over to Lisa's house."

"Lisa is barely at home. I am not about to let you spend another night alone over there, Lala. If you want, I'll sleep in the guest room."

"Whatever." I rolled my eyes and went to my woman cave.

Since I loved art, Stacks had a built-in art studio for me in the back. I played my Trey Songz 's CD and went to work. I must have been painting for a long time because Stacks came down to look for me.

"That looks hot," he said examining the portrait.

It was a picture of him holding a baby in a pink blanket.

"Thanks."

"You are going to have to give me this so I can hang it in my office."

"When it's done drying, you can have it."

I put the finishing touches on the painting then went to get prepared for bed.

Sending Lisa a text letting her know that I will be spending the night at home, I got in bed. Stacks' phone started to beep. It was a text from Amanda. I slid the screen and was pissed when I failed the passcode attempt. It made me mad that he would change it. Fed up with trying to figure out his passcode, I purposely entered the code incorrectly, locking him out for an hour.

"You need anything?" Stacks asked standing in the doorway, dressed in jeans and a hoody.

"No."

"I have to make a quick run. I'll be back."

"Okay."

He grabbed his phone, kissed me on the forehead, and the left. Getting out of bed, I made sure he was complexly gone before getting dressed and leaving behind him. I pulled up the "Track my iPhone" app and headed in the direction he was going. I watched where he was going before parking me car in the field across the street.

When he entered the diner, I waited five minutes before exiting my car. Peering through the diner window, he was seated alone before a female walked in from the back and sat in front of him. I couldn't believe he was doing all of this ranting and raving, and demanding I come back home, and he was still up to that sneaky shit.

If he wanted me so bad, he wouldn't have left me alone at home to meet up with some bitch. I watched them interact for a few minutes before leaving. I made my way towards Lisa's house. It was the first time that I decided to start making moves. First thing tomorrow morning, I was going to find me a house. Stacks and I were now history.

Chapter 24
Stacks

Leaving the 11th St. Diner, I was satisfied with the numbers Ralph were bringing in. He came to me with a new way to triple what we were already making, and I was all down for it. The only bad thing about my meeting was running into Amanda. I hadn't seen her since the day I went to her house to rough her up and for some weird reason she was under the impression that I missed her. Yeah right. If Ralph didn't come in when he did, I probably would have ended up in jail with domestic violence charges pending against me.

I swear I thought my eyes were playing tricks on me when I didn't see Lala's car parked in the driveway. I picked up my phone and dialed her number. When she didn't answer, I texted her.

Me: *Where are you?*

Wifey: *Lisa's house.*

Me: *Why did you leave after I told your ass not to?*

Wifey: *Go text that bitch you went to go meet at the diner, I'm going to bed, bye.*

Me: *It wasn't even like that, I went to go meet up with Ralph. That's why Lisa is home and not with him. Ask your girl.*

Wifey: *Good night Anthony!*

I wanted to drive over to Lisa's house and drag her hard headed ass home, but decided against it. Instead, I went inside to pump some iron in my weight room. I lifted weights until my body screamed from me to stop. Finally giving in, I went to the bathroom and showered.

I couldn't get my mind off of Lala. I had every intention on coming home and giving her ass a dose of act right, so she could get the hell out of her feelings and come home. When my thoughts got too much for me to bare I put on some clothes and hopped in my car. Parking in the parking lot, I walked inside Ink Daddy's to get tatted up.

"Welcome to Ink Daddy's, how can I help you?" the receptionist asked.

"I need your best tattoo artist to ink me up."

"Chink, someone is here requesting a tattoo from our best." She spoke into the intercom. A few minutes later, a guy that had tattoos on every inch of his body walked out of the back room.

"Follow me," he said, "What are you looking to get."

I handed him a picture of Lala.

"I want her on my back, but I want her holding a baby wrapped in a pink blanket."

"Okay, let me just draw this up and I'll be right with you."

It was eight am when he finally finished my tattoo. The shit hurt, but I needed it to calm my nerves. Looking at my back in the two-way mirror, he really proved to me why they called him the best of the best. The tattoo cost me seven hundred dollars, but I gave him a stack for a job well done.

I walked next door to a small little Spanish café and had some breakfast. The large cup of coffee with the three extra shots of espresso, plus this pressure I was smoking on had a nigga wide-awake. I took Lala's ring to a jeweler and had them update it. I had some pink and white diamonds added around the bands and made them engrave our names on the inside. I picked up a few pieces for my little princess as well. She was going to come out the womb draped in diamonds.

Finally making it back home, it was a little after ten am. I was going to shower, check on a few things then drag Lala's ass home by her tracks if I had to. I noticed an old white man knocking on the door. He was looking at the car, so I concluded it was the police. My heart suddenly sank to my stomach praying Lala was okay.

"How may I help you?" I asked the old pig.

"Yes. I'm looking for an Anthony Jones."

"And you are?"

"Officer Livingston with the City of Flint Police Department."

"Okay, so how can I, a residence of Miami, help you, a cop from Flint?" I asked praying like hell none of my old murders came back to bite me in the ass.

"Are you the grandson of Luther and Solise Jones?"

"Yes," I answered feeling my knees attempting to go weak.

"Can we go inside to talk?"

"Tell me out here," I said refusing to allow that pig in my house. I knew how they operated. They would do anything to get a glimpse of your lifestyle, so they'll have a reason to build a case against you.

"I'm sorry son, but they were murdered last month. When no one came to claim their body, we had them cremated. I didn't know they had any kinfolks until you're grandfather's daytime nurse was able to give us your information."

"Noooo!" I yelled out a gut-wrenching scream before breaking down and crying like a bitch. I didn't care how I looked at the moment. Those were the only parents I knew. I felt like everything I loved was being snatched from me. First my mother, then it was Donna and my twins, my brothers, now my grandparents.

"I want to show you something, maybe you could help us with figuring out who would want to do this to your grandparents," he said handing me some photos of the crime scene.

Paying close attention to the note, I knew it had to be Bear behind this, which only meant he found out about his brother and was out for blood.

"No. I have no idea. I can't think of anyone," I lied to the cop.

"Okay, if you can, here is my card," he said handing me the card "Oh, and before I forget, here."

He handed me two containers that held my grandparents' remains. I planned on having my jeweler make them some urns, so I could have them placed in a Columbarium. I wanted them to have a burial place of remembrance, so I could always visit them.

"Thanks."

I went inside the house and closed the door behind me. Placing the containers on the fireplace, I left to go be with the only person I had left in this world. I was happy when I didn't see Lisa's car in the driveway. Knocking on the door, I couldn't stop the tears from falling. I was really crushed.

"Stacks, what are you…"

"He took them from me," I cut her off.

I collapsed in her arms and broke down crying. She just sat there on the floor with me holding me. I felt so secure in her arms. I could feel the love radiating off her body and onto mine. After emptying my body of all its tears, I got up and picked her up off of the ground. I really didn't feel like talking, so I went in the guest room where she'd been staying in and went to sleep.

***

The smell of food woke me up out of my nap. There was a tray next to the bed with baked chicken, green beans, mash potatoes, and cornbread. A tall glass of juice, a cup of ice, and a bottle of Advil was on the tray as well. I took a few bites of the food, and then washed down two of the pills with the juice.

I laid my head back on the pillow and thought of the different ways I was going to kill Bear as soon as I found him. I was going to round up the guys and make a trip to Flint, Michigan. I was praying he would still be there and if not, I was taking down anyone close to him.

"Are you ready to talk about it?" Lala asked taking a seat on the bed.

I pulled her close to my chest and wrapped my arms around her.

"Bear killed my grandparents."

"Oh, I'm sorry to hear that."

"I need you."

"I'm here."

I slipped my tongue in her mouth and began sucking on it. It had been one whole month since I felt the insides of her walls. I was feeling sick, and I needed a dose of her to make me feel better. Lifting her shirt, I grabbed one of her breast and sucked on the nipple.

I pushed both of her breasts together and went back and forth between kissing then sucking each of them. Kissing my way down, I licked down her legs, stopping at her toes, taking each of them in my mouth. Spreading her legs I could see her juices spilling out of her like a cup of milk dripping on the floor.

Using my mouth, I licked and sucked her dry. Grabbing one of the melting ice cubes out of the cup, I used it to play with her clit. The warmth from her instantly melted the ice. Grabbing another one I stuck it in her hole, then sucked it out.

"Ooooooh papi eat this punani," she purred, pulling my head deeper in her pussy.

I ate her out until I felt a gush of liquid squirt out of her and into my mouth. Tugging at my pants, I released the beast. My dick doubled in size as the veins pierced through it anticipating the feeling of her pussy. Unable to resist any longer, I put my dick in her and held it there. I wanted to feel her walls tighten around my dick. She started grinding her hips on my dick, allowing her clit to rub against my shaft. She started grinding faster, letting me know that she was almost there. I played with her nipples, squeezing them causing more pleasure to shoot through her body.

Her body shuttered as her legs began to shake. Another flood of fluids leaked out of her coating my stomach. Getting up, she laid me down flat on the bed and began licking her cum off of my stomach. She lowered her head some more until she had my dick in her mouth. Gathering saliva in her mouth, she allowed it to drip down my dick sucking it all up making it real nasty. She played with that sensitive area I had between my balls forcing me to a premature orgasm. I filled her mouth up with my kids, and she swallowed them all.

She mounted my dick and began riding me nice and slow. Gripping her hips, I pulled her deeper into me. Laying her on her side, I put her in the 'L' position and started blowing her back out. Her pussy was so tantalizing that I was in a daze. It was so good I found myself drooling. I put in overtime in that pussy, and she paid me by squirting all over my dick soaking the sheets. I released myself in her then got up, and lifted her up with me.

I filled the tub with water and bubbles then sat her in it while I searched for fresh sheets to make the bed with. When I was done fixing the bed, I packed all her things in the suitcases and sat them by the door. Life was too short for us to be playing these games. She was either going to come home with me now or we were going to end it once and for all.

She rode me like a surfboard in the tub before we showered and got out.

"Get dressed we're going home," I said.

"Okay."

I'm glad she didn't put up a fight with me. I would have hated to have to put these paws on her or even worse end our relationship. I put her bags in my car and waited for her to come out. After an hour of waiting, I was about to go back in the house and cause hell until I saw her coming out with a plate of food and a cup of juice in her hand. I had to shake my head at how greedy she had become.

I couldn't complain though because our lil mama was doing her body well. She now had a visible baby bump, but it was her ass that looked nine months pregnant. Arriving home, I placed her suitcases in our bedroom and went to my office to hold a conference meeting with the guys. The following morning we were going to fly out to Flint. I didn't want to chance waiting and having him flee again.

*****

2 Pac's *Hail Mary*, blasted through my Studio Beats, as the plane finally landing in Flint.

"You ready to bleed the block?" Ralph asked.

"No doubt, these niggas about to feel me for real."

I picked up the rental, and we made our way straight to Bear's mom's house. This wasn't a vacation. We were on a mission to find that nigga. If I couldn't get to him, I would go fuck with that baby mama he thought no one knew of and his little sister. For the sake of their life, I just hoped and prayed he showed his fat ass.

We sat in the car in the same position for a day straight and there was still no sign of any movement from the house, so I drove to the upper east end to his baby mama's house and waited. I didn't plan on doing his son any harm; I just had to rough up his mother a little bit to get any information that would be beneficial to me.

We waited another night at Bear's baby mama house just to see if he would ever show up, but he never did. The nighttime sky took <u>over</u>; so we decided to go in. Picking the locks, we had access to the house. The foul scent of the house hit my nose and threatened to make me throw up everything I had for lunch.

Bear's three-year-old son was sleeping on the dirty floor next to needles, beer cans, and roaches. Feeling bad for the boy, I lifted him up, but the shit that was piled in his diapers weighed him down.

Walking inside of one of the bedrooms, the once beautiful Lacey was now a strung out whore. This was probably why he never mentioned he had a child. He was embarrassed. Either way, that was no excuse to have your child living in this nasty ass condition. Putting on my gloves, I slapped her in the face. The place looked contaminated as hell, so there was no way I was touching that bitch.

"What the fuck you doing in my house?" she screamed as she woke up.

"Bitch, get the fuck up!" Ralph said yanking her up by her frail arm.

She smiled a disgusting, toothless smile and sat up in the bed.

"Stacks, nice to see you again," she laughed.

"Let's cut the bullshit, Lacey, where's Bear?"

"Does it look like I know where he's at?"

"So, you telling me your baby daddy come back in town and don't stop by to check on your son?"

"He came and checked on Kenny, but I don't know where he's at. You know he works for Alan now. She picked up a half smoked cigarette off the floor and fired it up."

"What Alan?"

"Alan. The Alan y'all was beefing with, Nico's Alan."

"Word?" I was shocked, I knew this nigga was a snake, but I didn't know he was a rat, as well.

"Yup, word on the street is he killed Donna and your grandparents. Now he's teaming up with Alan and Nico to come after you."

"Not if I get to him first."

"Yeah, okay. You're on our turf nigga. You and your little sidekick out numbered."

Picking up a mirror she started doing lines, ignoring her baby's cry. I gave Ralph a head nod, and he slit her throat. Picking up the baby, I put him in the back of my car.

Driving to a nearby Wal-Mart, I bought him some diapers, wipes, clothes, shoes, and snacks. Cleaning him up the best way I could, I changed his diapers, clothes, and shoes and allowed him to finish up his snacks. When we got to the Catholic Church, I pulled the hood over my head and covered my eyes with a pair of shades. I sat him in a stroller in front of the church door then rang the bell. I sprinted back to the car. I sat and waited until I saw a nun pick him up, look around, and then take him inside.

Our next location was Bear's sister's house. The house looked quiet, so we made our way inside. JuJu, Bear's sister, was laid in bed asleep next to a man. Using the tip of my gun, I tapped her on the forehead.

"What in the world?" she screamed and jumped up.

Her reaction woke up the guy she was with. Ralph put him in a chokehold, putting him to sleep permanently.

"OMG, you killed my fiancé!" she cried running over to his limp body.

I allowed her to grieve over her lost before getting down to the reason of my visit.

"JuJu, have you seen Bear?" I asked.

"Fuck you, Stacks!"

"That's not the answer I want to hear."

"Go join your dead bitch in hell!!"

She struck a nerve in me when she said that. I slammed the butt of my gun into her face with so much force five of her teeth flew out.

"Be a good girl and you might live," I lied.

There was no way I was going to allow her to live after she disrespected Donna.

"Kill me now because I'm not telling you nothing about my brother, bitch ass nigga. You killed Dixon, and I can't wait until he makes you pay for it."

"How is that you and Dixon have more loyalty than your brother?" I asked while screwing the silencer tip on my gun. I was going to make her death a nasty one.

"Do what you came to do pussy ass nigga," she spat.

I nodded my head and Ralph and I both emptied our clip, aiming for her head only. The murder scene was a gruesome one.

Heading to a hotel, we decided to get some sleep, I had to take down Alan and Nico before heading home and I knew this was going to be a challenging job since they were now Flint's most powerful men. Before heading to bed, I sent Lala a text letting her know I loved her and to let my daughter know I loved her as well. I prayed that I could get this mission over with, so I could return home to my girls safely.

The following morning, I switched out the rental, and we laid low in the hotel until it was time to move. I didn't want to risk anyone seeing me that was why I preferred to move at night. When it was time to go, a bad feeling came over me. Something told me to leave it alone, but I shook it off. Waiting at the arcade where they had their main shop set up, I waited for one of them to leave alone.

A commotion outside woke us up out of our catnap. Nico was outside arguing with a crack head. He backhanded her, and she flew into a parked car. Laughing, he got in his car and pulled off. Allowing him to make it down the street, I started the car and followed him. He led us to a big house in the suburban area. We staked out the house until all of the lights were turned off. Hopping over the back gate, Ralph picked the back door's lock and just like that we were in his house. For someone who was swimming in money, his security system sucked.

"Move and I'll blow your head off." I felt the cold steel of the barrel of a gun in the back of my head.

Turning around, I was face to face with my long time enemy.

"Well, well, well, if it isn't Stacks," Nico smiled feeling victorious.

I smiled inside seeing Ralph out the corner of my eye slowly inching towards us.

"I planned on coming to Miami to pay you a visit and finish your ass off, but you made it that much easier for me by showing up to my house," he laughed. "I have to call Alan and let him know this."

The quick second that he turned his attention from me to his phone, Ralph took that as his opportunity to blow Nico's head off. His body hit the floor like a sack of potatoes, causing his gun to go off. I bent down, picked up his phone, and searched for Bear's number, but came up empty.

POW! POW! POW!

Three shots from behind us rang out. Nico's wife was standing behind the smoking gun. Pulling out my gun, I shot her two times in the head, and she fell next to her man, giving them the perfect Romeo and Juliet ending.

"Ughhh," Ralph groaned, holding his shoulder.

I carried him to the car, and then went back inside the house in search of something to start a fire with. Since Ralph's blood was stained in the carpet leaving his DNA, I had to burn the place down. Using some cooking oil, I poured it all over the floor leading up to the front door. I started the fire and watched it burn before hopping in the car and burning rubber.

The pilot did his best to patch up Ralph until we could make it back to Miami to see a doctor. I didn't want to risk being in Flint alone with an injured man. Lacey was right. I was outnumbered and I wasn't trying to play Russian roulette with my life.

When we landed, I had my private doctor meet up with us. The bullet went in and out, so he patched him up and gave him some pain pills. I brought him back to my house to allow him to rest in the guest bedroom.

"What happened to him?" Lala asked as soon as I walked in the room.

"He took a little hit to the shoulder. He'll survive no need to call Lisa and get her all worked up." I kissed her before going to take a shower.

"The nursery is finished," she said as soon as I entered the room.

"Come show it to me then."

We walked next door to the nursery and I was amazed. The room was painted pink, purple, and lime green. She had a care bear theme going on that really went well with the color scheme. All of the furniture in the room was white. Rubbing my hands across the grain of the wood, I could tell it was all top of the line. The baby's bathroom was nicely decorated in a pink zebra theme. All of her bath products were neatly stacked in the cabinets. These past three days I was gone, Lala was really putting in work.

"You like it?" she asked.

"I love it baby. You did a wonderful job. Did you think of any names yet?"

"No. Not yet. You?"

"Still thinking."

"Are you hungry?"

"Not really just tired."

I checked on Ralph, before Lala, and I retired in our room. I wasn't really able to sleep knowing I left Flint and Alan and Bear were still alive. I planned on sending a few of my guys to finish up Alan for me, but I wanted Bear brought back to me alive. I dreamed of the things I wanted to do to him, and I couldn't wait to put him through hell before sending him there.

Chapter 25
Ralph

I woke up to the smell of bacon and a horrible headache. I tried to get out of bed, but the pain in my shoulder caused me to lie back down.

"Baby, are you ok?" Lisa asked.

"Yeah, I'm good, just in some pain," I said. "Where are we?" I asked looking around at the unfamiliar room.

"Stacks' house. He brought you here to rest."

"That's what's up. Help me out of the bed, something smells real good, and I'm hungry."

She helped me out of bed, and into the shower. Careful not to wet the dressing on my arm, she soaped up every inch of my body. Rinsing me off with the showerhead, she got on the bed and gave a nigga some of that real good down south sloppy toppy.

Lisa handed me my clothes. I got dressed and we headed downstairs to have breakfast.

"What's good nigga, how you feeling?" Stacks asked.

"I'm straight. My shoulder hurt like a bitch though."

I sat at the table, and Lala sat a plate filled with eggs, grits, sausage, bacon, French toast, and home fries. Cleaning my plate, I washed everything with a glass of orange juice. Stacks and I went to his man cave while the ladies went to get their hair done.

"I'm mad that bitch caught me slipping." I grabbed the Xbox controller as we started a game of Madden. Stacks started to laugh.

"Yeah, that nigga Nico had him a gangster bitch."

"Well, I guess they're in hell riding for each other," I laughed.

We chopped it up and played a few more games before the girls came home.

Back at my place, I had just finished eating Lisa up for dinner, and she was getting ready to go home. Today was my boy, Tommy's birthday, and he was having a get together at KOD. Stacks was on lock down for the night so I got fresh in my Polo outfit, hopped in my Bentley, and was on my way to turn up.

My niggas and me were in V.I.P balling the hell out when a stripper by the name of Seduction came out on stage. I had a big booty bitch, name Orgasmic, on my lap popping her fat ass. I wasn't paying the dancer on stage no mind. The dancer that was all on me whispered in my ear that she wanted to take me to the backroom and fuck, but I had to decline.

I wasn't fucking with strippers like that. I made it rain on her, and then dismissed her ass. I had nothing against strippers. I just ain't want my girl doing it, unless it was for my eyes only.

"Damn that bitch bad," Tommy said.

By the time, I looked up she was done with her performance and exited the stage

"I'ma see if she's gon' comeback to our section and give me some birthday head."

I laughed at his extra eager ass and sent Lisa a text. Feeling my bladder fill up, I went to the bathroom to relieve myself. When I was done, I stopped by the bar to put in an order for some more bottles. I peeped some bitches in our V.I.P section and I wanted to make sure everybody had a drink.

I was no longer feeling the scene, so I left my credit card on file and told the bartender to charge everything to it. I was walking back to our V.I.P section to tell everybody I was out until I bumped into Lisa. She was dressed in a yellow fishnet short and bra set allowing every nigga up in here to stare at what was mine.

"Ralph, I can explain."

I ain't want to hear that shit! I made her go get her shit and dragged her ass out of the club. The air in the car was thick with tension as I drove to her house. When we got there, she jumped out of the car and ran to the door. I was hot on her heels pissed the fuck off.

As soon as the door closed, I backhanded her ass sending her flying to the floor. I picked her up by her throat with one hand and slapped her with the other.

"I'm sorry, please stop," she cried.

That shit only enraged me more. Smelling another nigga's scent on her body sent me over the edge. I slapped her around a few more times. I ripped the clothes off her body and demanded she go wash that damn cologne off her skin.

I rolled me a blunt and sat on her bed smoking it while waiting for her to return. I was mad at myself for hitting her, but she deserved that shit for keeping that from me. This explained why I could never get her to move in with me. The bitch was living a double life. How do you sit and tell someone you love them every night, but hide something so big like you shaking your ass for money every night for the next nigga?

The scent of fresh wild berries had entered the room before she did. I could see that her lip was swollen and her eyes were red and puffy. I got up and made her an ice pack then handed it to her.

"So, when were you going to tell me that you are a stripper?"

Silence.

"I know you hear me talking to you."

More silence.

I got up to leave. I wasn't playing games with a grown ass woman. If I wanted to play games, I'd play them with my two kids. When I finally made it to the door, she found her voice and started talking.

"I been stripping since I was young. Stripping is all I know. Stripping is what bought me this house, my cars, and is what has me financially stable at the moment. I never had anyone to take care of me, so I did it the best way I knew how. I was going to stop stripping when I met Bear and go to school, but he fucked me over so bad it was 'fuck you pay me'.

When I met you, you changed things around for me. You showed me how it felt to be loved again, but I was still scared. I held onto my job as my security blanket, something I could fall back on. I wanted to tell you millions of times, but couldn't bring myself to do it. I'm sorry."

I just looked at her and walked away. I couldn't deal with this shit right now. I completely understood in this world you had to get it how you live. She knew jumping into this with my occupation and not telling me would lead to something like this happening.

Hell, she even knew my life story so there was no reason why she should have kept that from me. In my book, that bitch was being sneaky. My phone beeped with a text from Kandi telling me she was in town visiting her family, and she wanted to meet up with me. I texted her my address and headed home.

Chapter 26

Bear

Tied to a chair, I was getting the living shit beaten out of me by Alan. He felt like I had something to do with the death of Nico and his sister, but that had Stacks written all over it. I didn't expect Stacks to come for me as hard as he did and because I underestimated him, my baby mama and sister were both dead, and my son was in foster care.

I felt myself fall in and out of consciousness as my flesh ripped as he severely beat me with a metal paddle. I must have blacked out because he was throwing ice-cold water in my face.

"Wake up! You'll get all the sleep you want when I kill you."

"I didn't have nothing to do with it. It was Stacks," I mumbled.

"What makes you so sure?"

"Because he killed my sister and baby's mom in retaliation for me killing his grandparents," I said. "Why would I kill Nico knowing that y'all holding my mother hostage."

"You got a point, but I'm going to make sure this doesn't' happen again."

He pulled a walkie talkie out of his back pocket and spoke into it.

"Bring her in," was the last thing I heard before I blacked out.

"Wake up fat boy you have a visitor," he said, slapping me in the face.

When my vision finally became clear, I saw my mom tied to a chair right across from me. I allowed the tears to fall as she began to receive the cruel beating before I blacked out again.

After he had beat her until she was black and blue, he handed me the gun.

"One of you have to die, it's either you or her."

He was saying either I kill myself or I kill my mother. I thought about it long and hard before stuffing the gun to my head. The only thing that stopped me from pulling the trigger was my infatuation with Stacks. He was going to be living his life while I was going to be the one buried six feet under. I was in too deep, and I didn't want to give up. Pulling the gun from my head, I whispered 'I love you' to my mom before blowing her brains out.

"You one cold ass nigga," he laughed.

I looked down at my mom's lifeless body, and I felt my face get hot. Not only did I want Stacks dead, I wanted Alan dead, as well. With any luck, they would do me a favor and just kill each other.

Alan left me tied to the chair and in the same room with my mother for two weeks straight. The smell of her body was unbearable. I threw up a few times. I was so dehydrated. I had to gather as much spit as I could in my mouth, and then swallow it. My pants were filled with my shit and pee due to me not being able to go to the restroom. I prayed for that gun so I could take myself out of this misery.

The next day, the doors finally opened and I was untied. I tried to get up, but my body was too weak. I gathered all of my strength then got up and walked out the door. Alan was standing by his car waiting for me.

"I wanted to kill you, but I need you. If any more of my people turnup dead, I am going to make you carve your son like a turkey, then I'm going to kill you personally myself."

He handed me a wad of cash.

"Go get yourself cleaned up, you stink. Meet me at the Arcade in two hours, so we can discuss how we are going to handle this Stacks situation and you better not have me waiting either."

He got in his car and left, leaving me standing in the dust. I walked to a nearby shopping center and bought me a few things that I would need. I felt embarrassed as hell walking around in the streets that I was well known in with a shitty ass. I wanted to slap the look off the cashier's face she was giving me as she rung up my things. Snatching my bags from her, I walked two blocks to a motel and got a room.

Peeling off the filthy clothes from my skin, I tied them in a bag and threw it down the hallway. I made sure the water was scorching hot before I stood under it and scrubbed my skin raw. I went through three bottles of Axe body wash trying to feel clean again.

Closing my eyes to wash my face, images of my mother's dead body began to haunt me. I got out of the shower, lined up my beard and got dressed in my new clothing. Spraying my body with the Nautica perfume, I felt much better now that I was looking and smelling like myself. My fresh new, out the box, pair of all white forces hit the pavement as I left the motel and waited for my cab to arrive.

Cab #664 finally pulled up. I gave him directions to the arcade and sat back until we got there.

"Twenty-three dollars," the taxi cab driver said giving me my price.

I paid him twenty-five dollars and made my way into the Arcade.

"You clean up nice," Alan laughed.

He motioned for me to have a seat.

"Now, tell me everything I need to know to take Stacks down."

I sat down in the chair and started running my mouth like the snitch I was.

Chapter 27

Ashley

Looking down at my baby boy, I examined his features. Nothing in him showed that he was half Columbian. I was baffled because the baby looked more like James than Pablo. I knew my math wasn't off, so I was confused as to why my baby was brown instead of tan. I was scared out of my mind that this was actually James' baby for the simple fact that Pablo would make good on his threat and kill me if he found out this baby wasn't his. I was also pissed because this baby was fatherless, so every hope I had of balling out on his father's expense was now dead.

"Why does the baby look fully black if his father is Spanish?" Amanda asked the same question that I was racking my brain trying to answer.

"He has to grow into his color I guess."

"So, how did you feel after giving birth?" She sat in the chair that was next to my hospital bed.

"I feel normal, just happy to be one person finally again."

"So where is his father?"

"He just left!" I snapped. I was getting annoyed with her interrogating me.

"Okay, no need to get hostile. It's just, I've been kicking it with you for the past month or so, and I never once seen him around."

"That's because he's married," I lied.

"Oh," she said. "Can I hold him?"

I gave her a blanket to drape across her before gently placing the baby in her arms. Although I was in a fucked up situation, it still didn't stop me from loving my son. The first time I held him I apologized to him over and over again for the fucked up things I did and said about him.

I just prayed that when Pablo finally decided to show up he would have mercy on me for leading him into believing this was his son. It was not like I did it intentionally, like with James. I actually did believe this was his child.

"What's up with you and Stacks?" I asked Amanda as she rocked with the baby in the rocking chair. Now that I dropped my load, I was ready to get real messy and fuck Lala's life up.

"I haven't really talked to him since the day he cursed me out at the diner."

"So, what do you plan on doing?"

"I don't know." She shrugged her shoulders.

I swear this girl was dumber than a bag of bricks. I had to teach this bitch everything on homewrecking one on one. I was busy working on my part of the plan, but I had to play in her head to make her do what I needed to be done so that everything can go as planned. I've been dating this FBI agent on and off. I've been dropping hints about Stacks and his drug operation. I needed this dumb bitch to get with the program.

"You have to be persistent if you want your man girl."

"What do you mean?"

"I mean, if you want Stacks, you have to go beyond all measures to get his attention. You leaving him alone gives him the opportunity to forget about you."

"So, what do I do?"

"Mess with Lala. The best way to get in a nigga's head is by messing with the main bitch. Trust me I know. That is why my baby daddy is currently going through a divorce."

"And you think this is going to work?"

"Trust me, I been a side bitch for years, I know the game like I know the back of my hand."

The baby began to cry and she handed him over to me, so I could feed him. I watched her as she allowed what I just told her to marinate in her head. She sat with me for a few more minutes before excusing herself, saying she would come back later to visit us. I just smiled knowing that she was going to go destruct some shit. When I was sure she was gone, I called up my cousin JT. He was one of Stacks' block boys. Ever since the death of his brother Red, he was just like me, out for blood.

"What's good, Ma," he answered.

"You do what I told you to do?"

"Done."

"Good. Talk to you later." I cut the phone call short as soon as the nurse came inside the room to get the baby.

I sat back and almost had an orgasm. That's how excited I was. Soon, Stacks' ass was going to be buried under the jail cell of a federal prison with a shitload of cases piled up against him. Maybe do us all a favor and kill himself once he finds out how horrible of a death Lala will die when I finally get my hands on her.

The nurse brought the baby back to me, and I held him in my arms. Looking in his eyes, I could see evidence of James. My best bet would be to hurry and put a plan in motion, getting as much money as JT and I could get from Stacks then fleeing Florida for good.

Chapter 28

Amanda

Taking Ashley's advice, I started following Stacks and Lala around. Every move they would make, I would do the same. I traded in the car that Stacks bought me for something else, and I even moved out of the house he gave me for a smaller apartment. I did not want him to know my whereabouts in case shit hit the fan, and he wanted to make good on his threats and kill me.

Parked in my new Nissan Altima, I sat and waited for any one of them to leave the house, so I could follow them. I saw Lisa's car pull in and a few moments later they both were getting into Lala's car and leaving. I waited a good five minutes before following them. I allowed them to park in the Aventura Mall's parking garage before parking a few parking spots down from them. When they were out of sight, I drove off in search of a Home Depot.

Returning, I pulled the hood over my head and made sure the parking garage was clear before making the damages to Lala's car. Satisfied with the masterpiece I created, I parked my car in the back and waited for them to return to the car.

Three long hours later I heard a scream. Looking up from my phone, I saw Lala staring at the damage in shock as Lisa yelled into the phone at someone. I laughed on the inside as I enjoyed the sight before me. The security guards came up to the parking garage, and Lala spoke with them. I wasn't worried about them finding out who I was because I was very careful.

I was about to pull off, but then changed my mind when I saw Stacks exit his car. I was so in love with that man, my heart skipped a beat whenever I saw him. I wanted to run over to him and talk to him, but under the circumstances, I decided not to. I was instantly filled with envy as I watched him hold and console her.

I badly wanted to be in her shoes and it was killing me. Feeling anxiety take over my body, I opened my pocketknife and started cutting myself. I laid my head back against the headrest and allowed the sensation of my stinging wounds to consume me.

Once my temporary high wore off, I snapped a few pictures that clearly showed Lala, and then I headed home. Before I could even stick my key inside the lock, my phone was ringing off the hook with calls from Stacks. I smiled, and answered the phone.

"Hello," I sweetly sang.

"Why the fuck are you messing with me, huh?"

"What are you talking about?" I was playing the dumb role.

"Don't play dumb! I know you fucked with Lala's car today?"

"How was I able to do that if I was on a date with my boyfriend?" I lied

"A date?"

"Yes, a date! Ain't nobody thinking about you anymore. I even sold the house you bought me and moved in with my boyfriend."

"Word?"

"Yes! Now, if you don't mind I got things to do!"

Hanging up the phone, I went and cleaned myself up. I was on my way to Loye's to see if he could hook my hair up like Lala's. I cropped her body out of the pictures only leaving the hair do. If I couldn't beat Lala, then I'd try to be her.

Chapter 29
Lisa

If Ralph wasn't going to hear me out, then I was going to pay him a visit and make him. I was looking sexy in a two-piece lace, satin boy short set. I tightly tied the trench coat around my waist and got in my car. I finally quit stripping for good.

Not because of Ralph, but because it was something I needed to do for myself. I had to understand that there was more in life than shaking my ass. I loved to write, maybe I'd write one of those vixen books, but instead of celebrities I'd expose all the real hood boss niggas.

Seeing Ralph's car parked out front made me real nervous. Butterflies instantly took over my stomach. Putting my emotions in check, I exited the car and walked up the driveway to the door. With every click of my heels against the pavement, my heart started beating faster and faster. With trembling hands, I used the key he gave me to open the door.

Making my way to his room, I heard moans. Removing my shoes so that I wouldn't alarm anyone, I followed those moans to the guest bedroom. Slightly pushing the door open, I saw the dude I'd been going crazy over these past few weeks fucking some bitch from the back. I watched her throw it back as he gave her that same dope dick he used to give me.

I knew it wasn't my place to get mad because we were no longer together, but I was hurt. The second guy that I gave my heart to shattered it.

"I guess this is why you were so quick to leave me," I said, startling them both.

"What are you doing here, Lisa?"

He pushed the girl to the side and grabbed his shorts off the ground, pulling them on.

"I came to give you this?" I said untying my trench coat. "And to beg you for another chance, but I see why you were so quick to leave me."

I tried my hardest to hold back the tears, but I couldn't. I allowed them to fall freely as they symbolized all the hurt and pain I was currently feeling.

"Baby don't cry."

"Baby?" I laughed. "Please don't try to make me feel as low as I'm feeling now."

I turned around and walked out of the same door I came in. Putting the key in the ignition, I pulled off driving with no destination in mind. My phone began to ring. The first ten calls were from Ralph and the next twenty were from Lala. I sent her a text letting her know I was okay and just clearing my head.

I didn't know what was wrong with me. Maybe I was cursed or some shit. Every man I ever fell in love with hurt me. Yes, part of what I went through with Ralph was my fault for not keeping it one hundred with him. I understood why he was mad, but for him to jump in the next bitch's pussy just a few weeks later without even giving me a chance to properly explain to him my actions, said a lot about his character.

For some odd reason, I ended up at the ice cream shop by the beach. I sat in the sand eating vanilla ice cream as I thought of Riley's pretty self. We had a spa date set for this weekend, and now I was stuck. I didn't want to let her down, but the situation between her father and I became messy.

"Can I sit here?" I looked up and saw Ralph. I wished I was packing so I could shoot his ass in the heart.

"It's a free country."

"Lisa, I'm sorry you had to see that."

"Are you really?"

"Yes. Even though we are no longer together I never meant to cause you any hurt."

"Yeah, I bet."

"No, for real, Lisa. The love I have for you is real, but my ego won't allow me to accept that you're a stripper."

"I quit! I came over to tell you that I quit and I was sorry. You didn't even give me a chance. Instead, you was knee deep in some pussy not giving a fuck about me or how I'm feeling!" I cried. "The damage is already done. You're dead to me!"

I slapped him in the face before getting in my car and pulling away.

Chapter 30
Lala

"Lala, hurry up or we're going to be late!" Stacks yelled.

I was in the room looking for my pearl set that would go perfectly with the all-white Vera Wang dress I was wearing. I didn't know where we were off to in such a rush. Earlier today, Stacks sent a make-up artist, hair stylist, and a nail tech and had them pamper me. He then came home with this all white dress and some white flats and asked me to hurry up and get dressed.

"Why don't you have on the flats I bought you?" he frowned.

"You can't wear flats with this dress, that's tacky."

"Well, I sure as hell don't want you walking around in heels eight months pregnant."

"These are not heels, they're wedges. Similar to flats, but a little higher," I smiled

"You're dressed, so what's taking you so long?"

"I can't find my pearls, how am I supposed to accessorize?"

"If you would have just hurried up and went with the flow, you would have seen that I had you covered."

He pulled out a red velvet box from behind his back and opened it. I started to drool over the beautiful diamonds that shined so bright. He clasps the necklace around my neck while placing soft kisses on it.

"Mmmm," I moaned.

I was ready to take off my dress and fuck him on the spot. Since I entered my third trimester, my sex drive was at an all-time high. If he sneezed, I would get hot, wet, and ready to fuck.

"A quickie before we go please?" I begged.

Raising my dress a little, he pulled out his dick. He held me up against the wall and fucked me real rough. I screamed out in pleasure as he bit down hard on my neck. Thrusting in and out of me with nice long strokes, he was driving my ass crazy. My eyes rolled to the back of my head as I squeezed my pussy muscles around his dick, sucking his dick dry before feeling a gush of fluids.

"You sure your water ain't break?" Stacks joked.

"Naw, you ain't stroking like that." I laughed.

He laid me on the bed and came back with rags to clean us up.

Adjusting my dress and touching up my make-up, I made sure my hair was still in place before we left. When we got to a red light, Stacks handed me a blindfold to put over my eyes. Making sure it was secure and blocked my vision, he made his way to our destination.

The car slowed down, and then came to a complete stop. I heard him open and close his door then come around to open mine.

"You better not fall or I'm kicking your ass for wearing them damn heels," he fussed, guiding me to wherever we were headed to.

Removing the blindfold, the whole room screamed out surprise at the top of their lungs. The ballroom was decorated in soft pink and white, with banners saying, "It's A Girl." I remembered Stacks asking me what I wanted to do for a baby shower, and I told him I really didn't want one.

"I'm going to get you," I said punching him in the arm before planting a soft kiss on his lips.

Lisa came over and placed a 'Mommy to be' sash around my body and a tiara on my head.

"I'ma get you, too! Why didn't you tell me?" I asked.

"Stacks threatened to kill me and I love my life."

"How are you holding up?"

"I'm good. Why you ask?"

I nodded my head towards Ralph and Kandi. They'd been really kicking it. He tried to bring her to my house one time, and I shut that shit down quick. I made him take her ass back to where she came from. Lisa was the only friend I needed. I ain't want no random bitch around me.

"Girl bye! I'm not on that," she lied.

"Girl you can fool every motherfucker in here, but you can't fool me."

"Today is your day, let's discuss this later."

Making my way to my table, it was decorated really nice. Two large containers filled with money were at the end of each of the tables as the guest filled the container with money. The security guards took them to the back to empty them. Everyone was enjoying themselves, eating, drinking, dancing, and stopping to play the baby shower games. Glancing at the gift table, I thought I was going to pass out. They had to rope off the whole back area just so there was room for the large load of gifts.

"Can I have this dance?" Stacks asked.

"Yes, you can."

Michael Jackson's slow version of *Love Never Felt So Good* was playing as we swayed to the beat.

"You know I love you right?" I said.

"Yes, I do and I love you more."

He leaned down and slipped his tongue in my mouth.

"When are you going to be my wife?"

"I don't have my ring."

He slipped the ring back on my finger. I examined it because it looked different.

"Did you get me a new ring?"

"No, I improved it, just like I improved myself. The ring symbolizes the changes I've made to become fully committed to you."

At that moment, I knew God had sent him down especially for me. He was everything I wanted in a man and more. Yes, we had our moments, but our relationship had last throughout all of the things we had been through.

Watching our friends and family celebrate the arrival of our baby girl brought tears to my eyes. This was what I prayed for when I used to lay in bed crying because James never made it home. God was answering my prayers all at once, and I felt my blessings overflowing.

The baby shower started to wind down as the waiters began to clean up. Stacks had to order a mini U-Haul truck just to carry the baby's belongings home. After saying our goodbyes and thanking everyone for coming, we made our way home.

"What's up with Ralph and Kandi?" I asked Stacks.

"None of your business, so stay out of it."

"I just wanted to know if he was really feeling her."

"He's coping. He really does love Lisa, but with men it's an ego thing. Things will fall in place. Like I said, stay out of it."

When we finally got home, Stacks stayed downstairs showing the men where to put the baby's things. I went to the master bathroom and ran some warm water. My feet were really killing me. Immersing in the warm water, I threw my head back and allowed the jets in the tub to massage my body. I felt a sharp pain shoot down my back to my vagina, but I ignored it. Another sharp pain hit me again, so I decided to get out of the tub.

As soon as my feet touched the floor another pain ran through my body leaving me doubled over in excruciating pain. Trying to stand all the way up, a gush of liquid came out of me.

"STACCCCCCCCCCCCKS!!!!!!!!!!" I yelled.

I heard him running up the stairs.

"Baby, you good?"

"No we have to get to the hospital, my water broke."

Running to the room, he grabbed me something to wear. After dressing me, he helped me get in the car before going back inside to get my bags.

"Oh, God, it hurts!" I yelled.

"Baby remember to breathe, you have to breathe."

"Fuck breathing, I want her out of me. NOW!"

Stacks floored it and heading to the hospital, stopping at a red light he pulled out his phone and called Lisa, then Ralph telling them to meet us at the hospital. Before another contraction hit me, the car was raided with bullets. Stacks was trying to drive away from them as fast as possible, and we ended up crashing into a tree, landing in a ditch.

"Lala, are you okay?" He asked.

"The head, I feel the pressure of the baby's head!" I cried.

"Okay, want you to relax for me and then push."

"I can't do it Stack. It hurts so badly."

"C'mon Lala push, please?"

I held on to Stacks' hand and started pushing with all my might. I noticed he was no longer saying anything. Looking over at him I could see he was a bloody mess, his eyes were closed as he laid his head against the window.

"Stacks baby wake up!" I panicked.

"I'm here baby I'm not going nowhere," he said. His voice was fading in and out.

After pushing our little girl out, I used some eyebrow scissors to cut the umbilical cord. Wrapping her in my bloody robe, I put her in Stacks' lap as I felt another pain shoot through my body. Preparing to push out the afterbirth, I started to push with everything in me. I felt something drop and then more crying. Looking down, it was another baby.

"Oh, God, Stacks it's another baby."

"Another baby?" he weakly asked.

"Yes, we have twins!"

He tried to smile, but started violently coughing up blood.

"My miracles," he said trying to reach for our son.

"Thank you, Lala, for giving me my kids. Let them know that daddy loves them. I love you too." He leaned his head back again, but this time he didn't budge as I tried to shake him.

"Stacks baby wake up please! I can't do this without you, please!" I cried right along with my kids.

Someone started breaking down the door. They grabbed me out of the car, then the babies, followed by Stacks.

"Ma'am, are you hurt?" the paramedic asked.

"Save him, please save him," I cried as my body began to tremble.

Watching his lifeless body on the pavement, I felt my knees get weak. I instantly became dizzy. The world started spinning as Stacks' final words to me replayed in my head. I couldn't believe this was happening to me. Hours ago we were so happy. It wasn't supposed to end like this!

I heard my babies crying in the far distance. I still wasn't able to wrap my head around the fact that I'd just given birth to twins. Watching the paramedics do all they could resuscitate him to no avail made my heart heavy. My stomach started to turn as I released all the food I ate today before collapsing on his body.

Bio

Lucinda John, is a 21-year-old resident of Florida. She first discovered her love for writing in fifth grade during the Fcats write. Since then, her imagination took a toll and she began to write short stories as a stress reliever. After reading numerous books from several of authors, that was when she realized that she should put her gift into use.

With the help of Myss Shan, she was able to release her first book Fallin' For A Boss, and Finessers all in one month! Aside from writing, Lucinda is a mother to three boys, Kamauri, Kaiden and Khyree. Although she had them young that didn't stop her from pursuing her dreams and making huge accomplishments.

'With God everything is possible' is the motto that motivated Lucinda to always aim high despite any circumstances.

Find the author on Facebook <u>Lucinda John</u>

Like our Facebook page <u>Shan Presents</u> or visit our website <u>www.shanpresents.com</u>

Text **SHAN** to **22828** to stay up to date with new releases, sneak peeks, and more...

CPSIA information can be obtained
at www.ICGtesting.com
Printed in the USA
LVOW02s0020070617
537193LV00009B/121/P